BY BECKY MONSON

How to Ruin the Holidays
Copyright © 2021 Becky Monson
Cover art by Angela Talley Smith

Other Books by Becky

Thirty-Two Going on Spinster
Thirty-Three Going on Girlfriend
Thirty-Four Going on Bride
Speak Now or Forever Hold Your Peace
Taking a Chance
Once Again in Christmas Falls
Just a Name
Just a Girl
The Accidental Text
The Love Potion

To my Auntie Frannie
Christmastime was always so fun with you.
I'll miss all the laugher and the inside jokes.
Until I can hug you again.

Chapter One

I like to rage crochet.

I've made some beautiful pieces in my anger. Like the scarf I'm currently wearing. It's got perfectly chained rows of a delicious hunter-green yarn. And it's full of my hate.

I'd originally started it for my on-again, off-again boyfriend, Steven. It was supposed to be a Christmas gift, one from my heart. Instead, I broke things off with him for the last time, finished the thing in one night (it was more than halfway done, but I'm also fast when I'm angry), and now wear it as a reminder that Heathen Steven is a big fat cheating jerk.

The reason I bring this up is because I could totally use some therapy crocheting right now, this time for dear old Dad. The stitches would be tight and in lime green and rust orange. His two least favorite colors. If only I'd brought my supplies with me.

"I don't know why you're fighting me on this; the ostrich room would suit her best," says Hattie, an older woman with light-pink hair. She and her sister, Irene—both widows, so I was told—own the bed-and-breakfast where I'm currently trying to get a room. Trying and failing.

"But the flamingo one has more va-va-voom," says Irene.

I wave my hand around, trying to get their attention. "Maybe we could flip a coin?" I say, hoping we can work this out quickly.

They ignore me. In fact, except for our initial conversation, I haven't been able to get a word in. Do they do this with all their guests? Or am I just the lucky recipient today?

They're both wearing sweaters that they probably got on a BOGO deal. Hattie—with the pink hair—her sweater is blue with snowflakes and Rudolph on the front. Irene's got on a red sweater with a snowman. He's wearing a top hat and green scarf and has a carrot nose with eyes and a smile made of coal. His stick arm is sporting a gloved hand that makes it look as if he's waving at me and saying, "Welcome to hell."

Hell, indeed.

After a flight with heavy turbulence—so terrible that I was compelled to send a text to my best friend, Cami, telling her that if I died she'd need to delete all the books on my Kindle—and a landing that made not one, but several people scream (including me), I arrived at the airport only to find that the SUV I'd rented had been mistakenly given to someone else. All they had left was something that looked like a blue wind-up toy, which then turned a two-hour drive into more than three, while I prayed to whatever deity would listen as I nearly lost control on some black ice not once, but twice.

All to bring me here—to the small town of Carole Cove, a place that looks like Christmas barfed all over it—to buy some land for my dad to prove to him that I'm ready to run an office

2

of my own. Maybe if I'd had the chance to do some research, I wouldn't have been so blindsided. But it all happened so fast.

I'm supposed to be anti-Christmas this year after a disaster of a Thanksgiving. I'm supposed to be planning a non-festive trip to the Virgin Islands with Cami right now. But nope—my dad sent me to this little town in Montana that looks like it's straight out of one of those campy holiday movies. And to add to that vibe, I've got a quirky pair of sisters fighting over which room I should have.

I've never been a big fan of those seasonal movies, but I've seen enough of them to know that this one would be about inn owners who don't get along and need a little holiday spirit to bring them together. And the title would be: *A Real Crap Christmas for Mara.*

The sisterly arguing is sort of my fault, though. If I had just told them why I was really here—if I had just been honest . . . But I was told that this town isn't keen on selling the land that my dad wants, even though the town is in debt and they need money because tourism has plummeted over the past couple of years. I figured I would need to keep a low profile until the auction takes place in three days. So when, upon arrival, Irene asked me why I was visiting (it wouldn't take a sleuth to figure out she's the town gossip) and insinuated I was one of the "real estate people" that have been "fishing" around the place, I told her I was here for pleasure. Which is only a half lie: I'm here for the *pleasure* of purchasing some land in this town.

Hearing this, the sisters started going on and on about how excited they were that someone as young as me would be here to see the town and maybe it was a sign that things were improving. And just as I was starting to feel extra guilty for the lie, the fight about which room to give me started up. I don't know exactly how long it's been going on, but it feels like an eternity.

I just want a room but I can tell that's not going to happen anytime soon, especially when Irene turns to me, her face an even deeper shade of pink, and says, "I'm so sorry, can you please excuse us for a second?"

Oh, I know that look. The gritted teeth, the wide eyes, the red face. We've moved from arguing slightly to a full-blown fight. I've given that look a time or two (or hundred) to my own brother. He's been the recipient of my rage scarves and hats a few times. I think he's actually the instigator of my hate crocheting. But that was back when it was even worth fighting him over something. Nowadays, I just roll my eyes — the same hazel-colored ones he has — and say, "Whatever."

The sisters move over to the corner of the room, where they escalate their whispering, and then there's a lot of finger pointing. At each other, toward the stairs where I'm assuming the rooms they rent are located, and, every once in a while, at me.

I yank my scarf down and pull my long dark-brown hair to the side to give my neck some air, take a seat in a red-and-green striped wingback chair, and take in my surroundings. This place is called the Mistletoe Bed-and-Breakfast, and it's one of only two places to stay in this stupid, tiny town.

The design aesthetic is lovely, starting with the large entryway boasting a grand staircase with a dark wood banister. The front room is filled with a few round tables and chairs (I'm assuming this is where the breakfast part of the bed-and-breakfast happens) and features a stone fireplace and wood paneling on the west and south walls.

I could list the heck out of this place and sell it in a hot second. After a few touch-ups . . . like removing the red-and-green plaid wallpaper on the north side of the front room and the Christmas decor that covers every possible square inch. The theme? Yes, it's mistletoe. It's dangling from every doorway and gathered to make garlands that hang from the ceiling and wind up the banister. The word "gaudy" comes to mind.

I decide that I'll just step outside and let them finish the fight, especially once Hattie becomes spitting mad—like there is actually spit. I could also use some fresh air since there's a very strong cinnamon smell going on in here.

I sling my purse over my shoulder and walk to the front door, opening it and nearly colliding with someone in my haste.

"Sorry," I say, looking at the ground as I blink a few times to get acclimated to the light streaming through the door and the feel of crisp late-afternoon air.

"No problem," says a deep, rumbling voice.

My eyes, which had traveled to the floor, move up from a pair of dark-brown very used work boots to dark jeans. Then to an expensive-looking brown leather biker jacket covering a nice pair of broad shoulders to a handsome face with a closed-mouth smile and bright crystal-blue eyes staring back at me.

"Sorry," I say again, shaking my head.

"Noel?" I hear one of the sisters say, and I look over my shoulder to see the fighting has stopped and both women are looking in our direction.

"Hi, ladies," he says.

"Are you here to help hang mistletoe?" asks Irene.

More mistletoe? Where the heck would they put it? From where I'm at, every square inch of this place looks covered.

Maybe they plan to wrap some around the toilet? Although it could already be there . . . I haven't had a chance to look.

"Sure, um . . . If I could . . . just . . ."

I swing my head back around and realize that I'm blocking the doorway.

"Sorry," I squeak out. That's apparently all I can say to this man.

I start to move to the side just as one of the sisters yells, "Stop!"

I freeze in my spot and then look over my shoulder again to see the two women hustling toward us.

"Look at you," Hattie says as they walk forward. Their faces are still a little pink, but both are now sporting grins.

"You're under the mistletoe," says Irene with a lift of her chin.

I look back toward the door, to the man they called Noel, and then up at the mistletoe hanging from the top of the doorframe between us.

Right. Of course there'd be mistletoe hanging in this doorway, and of course I'd be under it with a stranger. A handsome one, I'll admit, but he's still someone I never knew existed until right now. If this really were a cheesy holiday movie, I think I just had one of those meet-cute things. Where the woman and man, who are destined to be together, meet in a silly way. In fact, I'm pretty sure I've seen this exact thing happen in a show that Cami made me watch years ago.

But . . . this isn't a holiday movie—this is my life—and I'm not comfortable kissing someone I don't know. Even if his eyes are a lovely shade of blue . . . and the five o'clock shadow on his face has me wondering whether it would feel soft or scruffy if I touched it.

I shake my head to bring myself out of that train of thought. "That's . . . okay," I say, looking at the man and giving him one of those constipated smiles, like I'm not sure I should be smiling right now so it comes across as if I'm forcing it.

The sisters move to stand on either side of me, so now I'm flanked between them. "But you have to," says Hattie. "It's tradition." I look to my left and see Irene nodding her head in agreement.

My eyes travel back to the man currently standing on the other side of the door, and I recognize that he's also looking rather uncomfortable right now as he runs a hand through his light-brown hair, tousling it nicely.

"Come on," says Irene motioning toward the man and then toward me. "Just a peck on the cheek."

I look to each woman and then back to the man they called Noel. It's clear that although he's currently sporting an awkward smile—like he wants to do this about as much as I do—he's not going to unless I say it's okay.

I don't know if it's because of the smile or that little acknowledgment that the ball is in my court, but I give him a little shrug, as if to say, *Might as well.*

"I'll just . . ." Noel leans in, and before I can protest, he gives me a little kiss on my cheek. It's quick, but not enough for me to miss that he wears a spicy scented cologne and has soft lips. And yes, I can confirm that the scruff on his face is pretty soft.

The sisters clap after the encounter, with a little too much glee in my opinion. It was, after all, just a quick little peck.

"Come on in," says Hattie as they usher us both into the house and toward the front room that I'd just vacated in an attempt to get some fresh air.

"Settle something for us, Noel," says Irene as we walk back to the scene of the fight. She turns to Hattie and gives her a scowl. "Mara here is our very special guest, because she's here for pleasure and isn't one of those real estate cads that have taken over the town."

I hope I didn't flinch when she said I was here for pleasure. I mean, I did, but I hope it wasn't noticeable.

"Do you think she should have the ostrich room or the flamingo one?" she asks.

Noel looks to Hattie and then Irene, his face reminiscent of the mistletoe incident we just had. A very are-you-being-serious expression. He must know they are, because in the next second, he's got his shoulders back and looks like he's going to take this most ridiculous of questions seriously.

He looks at me, taking me in from head to toe. He puts a hand to his chin in a contemplative gesture. Oh yes, he's really working this. "I like every room in this place," he says. "But I'd have to say . . ." He pauses like he's weighing his options here, like he's not sure which sister will be the most upset with his answer. "I'd say the ostrich room is a solid choice." So apparently Hattie is not the one to trifle with. Good to know.

Irene's lips purse and she rolls her eyes, while Hattie gives a little fist pump of triumph.

"Let me get your key," she says, and she and Irene both go into the kitchen, leaving me alone with Noel.

"Sorry about that," he says, his voice indicating that he's not only talking about the mistletoe but also the ostrich experience I'm in for.

"I'm just grateful to finally have a room," I say. "You saved the day."

He laughs and then reaches up and rubs the back of his neck. "I think they're just excited to have a tourist here."

"Right," I say, letting my smile fall. I just have to make it three days and that's it. Then I'll be out of this town forever and will never have to set foot in Carole Cove again. Thank heaven for small miracles.

Hattie comes through the door, wiggling a key. "Let's get you to your room," she says, that crap-eating grin still on her face. I notice that Irene didn't come back with her.

"Well, thanks again," I say to Noel as I follow Hattie up the stairs toward the ostrich room.

Mistletoe and ostriches. This town gets an A-plus for weirdness. Oh yes, a lime-and-rust scarf for my dad is definitely going to happen.

Chapter Two

The ostrich room was underwhelming if I'm being honest. I thought it would be covered in them, like the main level of the inn was with the mistletoe. But it's tastefully done and has an almost European feel to it, with a four-poster bed taking up most of the space and a small bathroom with a stand-up shower. Bonus—the only Christmas decoration in sight is a small stuffed ostrich with a red scarf wrapped around its neck.

Thankfully the room doesn't look as though it's been barfed on by Christmas, and it has a pretty amazing view of the town, which wraps around a small lake. There are rolling foothills and evergreens as far as the eye can see. It's probably even more stunning when the aspen trees are full of leaves and the sun is glinting off the water. I suppose I can see why my dad wants some land here.

After settling in and shooting off a text to Michael—the attorney my dad hired to help me with Thursday's auction—who lives a couple of hours away in Missoula, I realize I haven't eaten anything since the measly pack of almonds on the plane, and I'm starving.

Armed with my Heathen Steven scarf and a cream-colored, double-breasted coat with large black buttons, I make my way out of the inn, waving to Hattie and Irene, and head toward the main street area of Carole Cove.

I take a big breath of the cold, crisp smell of winter air, put my wireless earbuds in, and turn on my favorite crime podcast. Some people listen to motivational music while they walk. I listen to deep-dive investigations into unsolved murders. I also watch them. I've even gotten Cami into one on YouTube called *Cosmetics and Crimes*, where a woman named Zoe puts on makeup while telling a story about a grisly murder. It's very entertaining.

Still, it's a bit jarring to be listening to a story about a woman who was buried in her own backyard as I walk down Main Street at dusk. It's a contradiction to the sight before me, with this Hallmark-looking town and the thousands of twinkling lights covering all the buildings, light posts, and trees that line the sidewalk. If I had come here last year, maybe I wouldn't be so bah humbug about it. It might have even seemed a little magical, with the garlands running along the awnings of every store and the holiday-filled window displays. But as it stands, it's all just pouring salt into the holiday wound I'm carrying around.

Because I know someone else who will hate this as much as I do, I turn my back toward the town, pull the phone out of my pocket, and switch my camera so it's in selfie mode. Snapping a picture of myself with a big silly grin and the town in the background, I send it off to Cami with a text saying, "I've landed in a Hallmark town."

My phone dings almost instantly.

Cami: Gross

I send her back a laughing emoji. I would expect nothing less from her. It wasn't that long ago Cami would have had the opposite reply. Christmas used to be her favorite holiday. In fact, she lives in the town of Aspen Lake, which has a large downtown area with holiday movie vibes of its own. Not quite as much of a Hallmark look as this town has, but I'm not sure anything could top this.

Cami used to be very over-the-top about Christmas. But that was before the *incident*. The one where she found her husband—my own *brother*—under her decorated tree with another woman. It's one of those moments that makes a sister proud. *So stinking proud.* Let's just say Ben got a very ugly hate-filled hat that year as his gift. And as a bonus I didn't even plan on, it didn't fit his big, stupid head.

My mom was so disappointed—not in my hat, but in Ben. She loved Cami, still does. And my dad . . . well, that's another story—one that ends with "the apple doesn't fall far from the tree." Hence the reason why my mother is currently living in the west wing of my parents' home. Which is . . . also another story. One I'm trying not to think about right now.

Cami and Ben's marriage ended soon after, and I took Cami in the divorce. Obviously, Ben is my brother and only sibling, so I couldn't write him off completely. I kind of wish I could, though. His new wife—the woman he cheated with—is a real piece of work.

Her name is Claudia Cann and she's just . . . obnoxious. She's an influencer on Instagram and super full of herself. She's also a huge part of the reason my Thanksgiving was ruined, and therefore my Christmas. Claudia *Cann* kiss my butt. Besides rage crocheting, I have another hobby using Claudia's email to register for different companies—ones I know she'll find offensive. Like AARP, since she's not old enough for that yet. Or plastic surgeons' lists, since she claims to abhor surgical enhancements (although Cami and I have our suspicions). Every time she complains about getting so many emails, I put her on another list. It brings me much joy.

Cami's a bit of an influencer herself. After she posted wedding pictures she'd cropped Ben out of or doctored to show her anger—like Ben holding his bloody head in his arms while Cami shoved it full of wedding cake—people went wild for it. She now has a very popular website with a lot of followers where she blogs about relationships (and how to avoid them at all costs) and helps other people crop their exes out of their pictures. The best part is it's all been a huge slap in the face to Ben, which also brings me joy. Serves him right.

"Well, hello there," says a man as he walks toward me. I dart a look to my left and right, wondering who he's talking to before I realize it's me.

"Uh . . . hi," I say, pulling one of my earbuds out.

"Can I help you find something?" he asks, adjusting his red-and-green bow tie. He has black square-framed glasses and a full head of white hair. He's probably around my dad's age.

"Um . . . no. Thanks. Just having a look around," I say.

"Mayor Holiday, at your service," he says, holding out a hand clad in a black leather glove.

"Mara," I say, reaching out for a firm shake. "Did you say your last name was Holiday?"

He gives me a closed-mouth smile and, releasing my hand, adjusts his bow tie again. "You heard correctly. Fitting, isn't it?" he says, reaching his hands out toward the town.

"Very," I say. A Christmas town with a mayor named Holiday? Oh, Cami is going to hate this.

"First time in our little town?" he asks.

I nod my head. "Yep. First time."

He eyes me, studying my face for a brief second. "Work or pleasure?"

"Pleasure," I say, keeping up my ruse. I have to now, especially with what happened at the inn and the fact this is a small town and I'm sure word travels fast. Three days—I just have to make it three days.

"Excellent," he says. "So where are you visiting from . . . Mara, right?"

"Yes, you've got it. I'm here from Carson City."

"Nevada?"

"That's the one," I say. The *only* one. In fact, the only reason most people have heard about the city I was raised in is because it's the capital of Nevada and we all had to memorize states and capitals in elementary school. That, and you have to drive through it if you plan to go to Aspen Lake, which is only thirty minutes west of Carson City and boasts lake life during the summer and skiing during the winter.

"Well, Mara, an official welcome to Carole Cove," he says. "I hope you enjoy your stay here."

"Thank you."

"If you need anything, you let me know, okay?"

"Will do," I say, wondering if he'll be so congenial when he sees me at the land auction happening in three days.

He gives me a little wave goodbye and walks toward the bed-and-breakfast, stopping to pick up a piece of paper off the ground and tossing it in a black steel trash can as he goes.

I shake my head as I walk in the opposite direction, passing by a store called Garland Mercantile, then Rudolph's Barbershop, until I see a powder-blue door with a sign above it that says *The Cheerful Baker*. It has a window scape filled with gorgeously decorated Christmas cakes and cupcakes, and my stomach does a little jump at the sight.

When I open the door and the sweet scents of yeast and sugar waft out, I know I've made the right decision. Inside, the whole place is covered in the same blue as the door, and the floor is a black-and-white checkered pattern, giving the space a very 1950s vibe. It's decorated for the season, of course, but done in mostly red with some green accents. The name is very fitting. My Grinch heart grew one size bigger just by walking through the door.

No one is manning the counter, so I take time to check out all the delicious-looking cookies, pastries, cakes, and pies in the display case.

"Hello," says a brash-sounding voice, coming from a woman who's just entered through a swinging door behind the counter. She's got on a pair of black pants, a white buttoned-up collared shirt, and a blue-and-red striped apron that matches the place. "Can I help you."

This was not said in the form of a question.

Before me is a petite older woman with dyed-red hair and a pointy nose. She's got a very distinct scowl. I obviously don't know her, but my first impression is that she doesn't seem as cheerful as the name of the place would suggest.

"Um . . . hello," I say, feeling suddenly nervous. She just has an air about her. "What do you suggest?" I point toward the display case separating us.

She peers down her nose at me, which is kind of hard to do since she's shorter than I am, but she's managing to really nail the look. "Dunno—I'm not your stomach, am I?" She practically spits out the words.

Right. Now I'm thinking that maybe she needs to rethink the whole cheerful baker thing. The Curmudgeonly Baker might be more fitting. Is there a comment card where I can suggest this?

If I could, I'd make her a scarf in neon yellow. It's the only color I can think of that wouldn't go with this place. *Do not offend the pastry lady,* my stomach warns.

"Okay, I guess I'll take one of those," I say, pointing toward a row of chocolate-filled croissants.

Mean Baker Lady eyes me again, and then with jerky movements, she pulls out a piece of precut wax paper from a box on the counter and shoves open the door of the display case, making the whole thing rattle a little as she does. She snags one of the chocolate croissants and then shuts the door. I reach across the counter to grab it, but she holds it close to her body.

"You're not one of them real estate investors, are you?" she asks, her faced angled to the side, her glare questioning.

"Uh, no," I say. I blink rapidly. I feel like this woman can see into my soul. I really don't like to lie, even though I've done so three times now. I mean, I've been known to exaggerate a bit, especially in my business. *This is the perfect neighborhood! The location is optimal!* We call it *puffing* in the real estate biz. But all this outright lying is kind of making me itchy.

Still, right now, it's clear that I have to keep going with it. Not just because I want the croissant she's holding, but also because I don't have a death wish—and wonder whether, if she knew the truth, I might end up locked in her freezer.

It's possible that I may listen to too many crime podcasts.

"There's been a lot of your kind in this town," she continues. "And I don't make pastries for land hogs. No one is coming in and ruining my town with their big corporations." She takes a step away from the counter, keeping the pastry even farther out of reach.

Is she for real? Land hogs? I may be here for the land, but my dad has no intention of building any corporations on it. He said he wanted it for posterity or something. Not that I'd ever build a house out here in nowheresville if I ever inherited the land. I can't live anywhere where the closest Target is two hours away. No thank you.

So essentially, I'm here to save the town, not ruin it. The holiday movie version of this story would be *The Real Estate Agent Who Saved Carole Cove*. Or something better than that. I don't think this woman would believe me if I told her, though.

"No, I'm just visiting," I say, giving her a little smile for emphasis.

She squints her eyes as if she doesn't believe me. Do real estate agents have a look I'm unaware of? Because I feel like I'm just a regular gal. I've never given off the vibe of being a schmoozer like my dad and brother sometimes do.

The not-so-cheerful baker stares at me, and I stare back. I could walk out right now and find somewhere else to spend my money, but the thing is . . . this is all feeling a little bit like a challenge, and I've never been one to walk away from a challenge. I also *really* want that croissant.

It's time to pull out the big guns. I roll my shoulders back and look the woman in the eyes. "How did the real estate agent help his wife fall asleep?" I ask her, and she squints her eyes for a few seconds but then gives me a quick upward tip of her chin, nonverbally telling me to go on. "He told her about what he does for work."

The curmudgeonly baker doesn't move. She stays put, that same squinty-eyed look on her face. Frozen as if she's been carved out of stone. I give it a few seconds to let my joke land where I'm hoping it will.

I didn't know this about myself, but apparently I will do a lot of things for a flaky, chocolaty pastry. Including making fun of what I do for work. I'm actually armed with a bunch of these kinds of jokes since I memorized them to roast my brother, Ben. We may do the same thing for work, but it just felt like a little sister thing to do. Of course, this was BC—*before Claudia*. I don't make jokes with Ben anymore.

Baker Lady continues her staring, and just as I'm about to give up and leave this place pastry-free, I hear a little snort. Just one quick one. And then I see her lips pull up into a tiny smile. It's almost microscopic, but I see it.

"That's a good one," she says. "I need to write it down."

She sets the pastry down on the counter just out of my reach and goes over to an old-fashioned cash register and pulls out some receipt paper. "Tell me that one again?" She grabs a pencil and writes it down as I retell it.

"Excellent," she says, setting the pencil down. She's still not even close to cheerful, but she does seem a little lighter as she walks over and picks up the pastry and hands it to me. "For that joke, this one's on the house."

"Oh, no . . . I—"

"Don't you go arguing with me, girl. I don't offer free pastries to just anyone." She points a finger at me, her scowl back.

Guilt slips down my spine, like a slow-dripping paint drop. I lied to this woman, and now she's giving me a free pastry. I did give her a joke, though. She just didn't know it was at my own expense. Oh gosh . . . my conscience, or a chocolate croissant? This is hard.

"Thank you," I say in the next second, reaching up and grabbing the wax paper–covered pastry. To be honest, it wasn't that hard of a decision. I'll be out of this town soon and will probably never have a chance to eat here again. A hungry girl's gotta do what a hungry girl's gotta do.

My lie is justified within the first bite. I don't know if I've ever had anything better in my life.

I go to leave, and just as I open the door, there's someone coming in at the same time and we nearly collide.

"We meet again," says a man's voice, and I look up to see the same guy from earlier today. The one from the inn. The tip of his nose is red from the frigid temperatures outside, and he's holding a set of tools in his hand.

"So we do," I say, giving him a smile. Is it weird that I feel relief to see a face I recognize? Even if I've only just met this person?

"How did you end up liking the ostrich room?" he asks, the corner of his lips pulled up slightly.

"It was . . . kind of underwhelming," I say.

He chuckles. "Really?"

"I mean, it was lovely, but there wasn't one sprig of mistletoe anywhere."

His chuckle turns into a laugh. It's a nice one. Low and warm.

"Well, I can tell Irene and Hattie to put some in there, if you'd like."

"No," I say, holding out a hand to stop this idea. "I think I'll be okay without it."

"I'm Noel, by the way." He reaches out the gloved hand that's not carrying the tool set.

"Mara," I say, taking his hand in mine.

"So, can I . . . uh . . ." He inclines his head toward the store that he's trying to enter, where I'm once again blocking the doorway.

"Right," I say, taking a step to my right so he can enter.

"Stop right there!" says the ornery baker before Noel can step foot into the store.

I freeze in my spot, wondering if—somehow in the few seconds it took me to attempt to leave her place—she's figured me out and knows why I'm really in this town. I've had only one encounter with this woman, and I was hoping it would be my last.

I hear her shuffle over toward us, and I slowly turn my head to see her standing on my left with Noel still in the doorway.

"It's tradition," she says with a head tilt toward the door casing that Noel and I were just standing on either side of.

I close my eyes and shake my head. I know what will be there when I look up. Noel lets out a little snort.

I open my eyes and look up, and there it is. A little sprig of mistletoe. This time it's not dangling, but rather taped to the top of the doorframe. Easy to miss.

I look at Noel and see him smiling at me. It's a closed-mouth smirk, but it makes two very distinct dimples pop out.

Then I look over to the baker and see the scowl that's on her face. I don't know if I can say no to this woman, much less argue with her about it.

I decide to give in. Besides, we've already done this. At this point, it's like old hat with Noel and me.

"Tradition," I say, and Noel just gives a little nod. "Okay, then."

I lean in toward Noel, and just like before, he gives me a quick kiss on the cheek. I get a whiff of that spicy cologne again. His lips feel cold on my warm face, and his scruff tickles the side of my jaw.

There's no clapping from the rude baker like from Irene and Hattie earlier—just a simple nod and a gruff, "Come on in, Noel. You here to fix that leaky pipe in my sink?"

"Sure am," he says as I move aside and he walks in. He holds the tool set up as proof.

"Well, come on, then; we don't have all day." She turns and walks toward the back.

Noel gives me an eyebrow raise, and with that little gesture, I gather that he feels the same as I do about the baker. Maybe she scares everyone in this town.

I turn to go, but before I walk out the door, I look over my shoulder at Noel and the baker woman, and I find that Noel is doing the same thing—looking over his shoulder at me. We both smile, and I give him a little wave and then leave.

"I'm not kidding. This place feels like I've walked right onto a Hallmark movie set," I say to Cami on the phone later that night. I'm lying on my stomach on my bed, chin in my hands, the stuffed ostrich I've named Ollie staring at me with his glassy eyes.

"I don't know—it sounds pretty entertaining," Cami says. "You've got the fighting sisters at the inn, a mayor named Holiday, a baker with an attitude who's in need of a little Christmas spirit."

"And a man I've been caught under the mistletoe with not once, but twice."

"Yes, you've mentioned that," she says with a knowing tone to her voice. "I believe you said there was facial hair, and it was soft."

"Oh, shut up," I say, annoyed with myself for bringing it up again. I'm tired and my brain is short-circuiting.

"He must be cute, the mistletoe guy," she says, now with a teasing tone.

"Whatever. He's . . . he's a small-town bumpkin."

"A bumpkin with sexy facial scruff. Also, only eighty-year-olds say 'bumpkin.'"

"Shut up. And I didn't say the scruff was sexy," I tell her, my voice pitching up. Although it was a little sexy. In another world, one where I'm not in Christmas hell, I would definitely find Noel attractive at first glance.

"You didn't? Maybe it was your tone, then. Wait!" she says, her voice excited. "If you really are in a movie, then sexy facial scruff guy is the small-town store owner looking for love, and you're the big-city woman who's down on romance and all things Christmas, and he's supposed to take you around the town and show you the true meaning of the holidays."

"You can shut up now," I say, my voice flat. "You're ridiculous. And besides, I don't think Noel owns a store. He's like the town handyman or something."

"Oh, his name is Noel, is it?" Cami says. I know exactly what her face looks like right now. It's cocked to the side and accusatory. "That's quite the Christmas name. Isn't that fitting."

"Stop it. I hadn't even put that together." Funny that I didn't even realize it. Just another thing to add to the list. A handyman named Noel in a Christmas town.

"Well, you better tell me everything that happens. Let me know if you meet a prince in disguise. Or if they're trying to organize a big talent show to earn money for the town center. Or a big corporate guy who leaves the hustle of the big city to open a coffee shop. Or kids who play matchmaker for their single parent."

"Oh gosh," I say, laughing. "Those movies are so cliché."

Cami sighs. "And I used to love them."

"I'm glad you aren't torturing me by making me watch them with you anymore. It was hella bad."

"Hella? Next level hell, then?" she quips, making fun of the word I sometimes use when I find something to be worse than hell. "Well, it sounds like you're living one right now. You better hurry up and get out of that town before you get C-word cooties," she says.

"I thought you were calling it Christmas now?"

"Yeah, old habits die hard," she says. "Besides, I'm easing my way back into the holiday."

"And I'm trying to run away from it, but it's being shoved in my face. This is really unfair," I say. "You should be hating on it with me."

"Well, I still hate it. There's just less hate in my heart these days."

This makes me smile. The sting of my brother's betrayal has been overshadowed by a certain someone who's come into Cami's life recently, and I couldn't be happier for her. Even if the person used to be my brother's best friend — Noah. It's kind of complicated, and I'm still getting used to the idea, if I'm being honest. Cami's happiness is the most important part, though.

We say our goodbyes after Cami gets a call on the other line; I know by the smile in her voice that it's Noah, so I let her go. After we hang up, I roll onto my back and look up at the ceiling.

I only have to make it three nights in this place. I'll just keep a low profile and stay in my room as much as I can. No Christmas cooties for me.

Chapter Three

"This auction is important to me, kiddo," my dad says to me over the phone the next morning. I'm in my room at the inn, just finishing my makeup and running a brush through my long brown hair.

"I know, and I'm on it," I say, with as much confidence as I can muster. "I have no idea what I'm up against, though."

"You've got a lot riding on this. The office here in Carson City is yours for the taking."

"I'm up to the task," I say. I contemplate adding a "Sir, yes sir!" But Jay Scott is more the serious type.

A tinge of nervousness travels down my spine. What if I can't do it? I'm armed with a budget that should outdo anyone here. But what if it doesn't? Will I never get to run an office and forever be in Ben's shadow?

"Did Ben have to prove himself like this?" I ask my dad, curiosity getting the best of me. It's always felt like Ben has had things handed to him, and I've had to work for it.

"Of course," he says, without even a pause. "He got me the lot for the house."

Right, that was a coveted lot, which Ben won in a bidding war. I'm still not sure how he did it and I don't think I want to know. Regardless, Ben's now running the California side of Aspen Lake, so he made it happen.

"Why do you want this land again?" I ask, just to hear him say it again.

"I told you. It's for our family," he says, his voice indicating a slight bit of irritation. I've asked him this quite a few times, after all.

"Well, don't save any of it for me," I say. "This town is strange. You were right about them not wanting to sell."

"Yes," he says, and I can picture him doing the stoic dip of his chin he often does. "Best to keep a low profile."

"That's what I'm doing. They'll be happy when I win though, since we're essentially saving this town."

"I suppose we are."

"How's Mom?" I ask, keeping my voice breezy, treading lightly. Like you would do with an acquaintance. *How's ole Joe doing?* The real question I want to ask is whether she's moved back into the master bedroom.

My parents are all about putting on airs; Ben too, which makes me wonder if I was switched at birth, because I refuse to do any of that. What you see is what you get with me. Well, except for this town, which thinks I'm here as just a tourist.

"She's fine," he says, his voice curt.

So much in that two-word sentence. I better call her soon. She's clearly *not* fine, and my dreams of Mommy and Daddy getting back together feel like they're slipping out of my grasp.

Even though sometimes I wonder if she'd be better off. My family relationships are tenuous, at best.

We say goodbye and hang up, and it's at this point that I realize I need some caffeine. The real stuff—not the watered-down coffee Hattie and Irene offered with breakfast. The food itself was wonderful, though. Light, fluffy pancakes and crispy bacon. Homemade raspberry-peach jam on the side.

Caffeine is definitely needed right now, and I know where I'll go. In my perusal of Main Street yesterday evening, I saw a cute little place called the Merry Little Coffee Shop. I wanted to check it out but it was already closed for the night. I couldn't see inside, but I'm sure it's just as Christmas-y as everything else in this town. If they can make me a yummy latte, then I'll deal with it.

I put on my Heathen Steven scarf, over the new leopard-print coat Cami had unsuccessfully stopped me from buying at a Black Friday sale, and I make my way down to Main Street toward the coffee shop, looking for any other crazy things I can tell Cami about this town.

Nothing really jumps out. In fact, as I walk to my intended destination, a crime podcast playing in my ears, it's feeling a little magical here: the midmorning air is crisp, and the layer of snow that fell last night twinkles like glitter where the sun hits it. The part of the lake that's not frozen sparkles under the sun, too, and I feel like a little part of me—a tiny part—hates this place a little less than it did yesterday. Especially when I open the door to the coffee shop and am pleasantly surprised to find that it looks oddly normal. Not like it stepped out of a Christmas movie—no festive barf all over it—but more like a place I'd find back home.

The room is small but cozy and rectangular shaped, with a long butcher block counter to my right that a couple of people are working behind. I can hear the familiar sounds of an espresso machine, which makes my heart go all aflutter. To my left there are some tables and chairs, which are mostly filled with people drinking their coffee, either alone or in small groups. On the wall by the front door hangs a portrait of a man with dusty-blond hair and a nice smile with a plaque underneath that says, *In memory of Kyle Mitchell.*

The walls are a dark forest green, with light wood accents and a shelf running along the left wall, holding tasteful Christmas decor. The name fits the interior—it's quite merry. But not too merry. Let's just hope the people working here fit the name, too, and aren't like the rotten baker down the street whose demeanor is nowhere near as cheerful as the name of her shop would indicate.

I get in the line, about three people deep, and decide that if I get sick of my room back at the Mistletoe, I'll just plop myself here at a table with my laptop. It feels like home here. Cozy and comfortable and most importantly: normal.

"Well, I think it's downright rude," says a loud voice that can be heard over the din of the room.

And just like that, my normal bubble pops.

I'd know that voice anywhere. I only heard it once, but it was burned on my brain. I'd just thought of her too—maybe I conjured her up like a magic spell or something. I lean a little to the right, past the heads of the people in front of me and see a small-framed woman wearing navy pants and a white buttoned-up shirt by the counter. It's definitely her, the Very Uncheerful Baker.

I can't see her face, but her posture is stern, not unlike how she was with me yesterday.

". . . stealing my business," I catch her saying, as she points a finger at the woman who's manning the order station.

"We're not stealing your business," says the woman, who's looking a little haggard, judging by the bags under her eyes and the overly messy bun atop her head. "It's just muffins, breads, and some breakfast sandwiches."

"It's baked goods, and I'm the resident baker around here," mean baker lady says, directing a thumb at herself.

"I promise, we're not trying to take your business. It's not even the same baked goods you sell."

Baker lady shakes her head. "And then you're letting the enemy in here." She twists the top half of her body around and points over to the corner of the shop where there's a table of four men sitting, coffee cups in front of them, chatting to each other.

"We can't control who comes in here," says the woman behind the counter, exasperation now in her voice.

"Well, I do. I don't serve any of them land hogs."

The woman takes a big visible breath. "Gladys, I've got customers behind you. Can we talk about this later?"

The baker throws her shoulders back. "You can count on it," she says, and then she stalks out of the shop.

The woman at the order station takes another deep breath, lets her shoulders sag for just a moment, and then lifts them back up with a smile plastered on her face as she says, "How can I help you?" to the next person in line.

I look back over my shoulder at the table of men sitting in the corner. This must be some of the competition. For as annoying as she is, the rude baker might have just done me a favor.

By the way they're dressed, you can tell they're not here for fun. They weren't in suits or anything, but definitely business casual. Not like the rest of the crowd in here with their knitted hats and vacation vibes. I look very much the part of the tourist in my outfit, which was unintentional, but it's probably helping my case.

Maybe, after I get my coffee, I should go sit over in that area. Not close, but close enough. The auction for the land is a minimum bid one, which means the seller — which in this case is the town — has set a minimum price that must be met before the property can sell. I'm armed with substantially more to offer than the minimum, but it would be nice to know the amount others are prepared to bid. Essentially, any info I might get on what others are thinking will only help my case.

"What can I get you?" the woman manning the order station says when it's my turn. She looks even more tired up close. Like she's had a rough night, or maybe month.

"Uh, yeah . . . ," I say, looking at the menu behind her. "I think I'd like to try the caramel-and-hazelnut latte."

"Good choice," she says, her mouth playing at a smile.

"Rough day?" I ask as I hand her my debit card.

Her shoulders sag, just a little. "You could say that." She takes the card and slides it down the scanner on the register.

"The woman?" I say, pointing toward the door where the baker lady had vacated just a few minutes before.

"Oh, Gladys? That's the least of my worries," she says, with a quick glance at the ceiling. "She's been coming in here every day for a while now. Ever since we added some other menu items besides coffee. She's harmless, really."

I'm not too sure of that. I only met her yesterday, but I think it's safe to assume that she could burn the place down if she got too angry.

"What brings you to town?"

"Just doing the tourist thing," I say. The lie rolls off my tongue now; I don't even have to think about it. Besides, I feel touristy right now, spending time in the town.

"Well, welcome," she says as she hands me my card back. "I'm Ivy, by the way."

"Mara," I say.

"Well, Mara, your drink will be ready at the end of the counter." She nods her head toward a teenager at the other end who's busy making beverages. "I hope you enjoy your stay here, and if you need anything, please let me know."

Well, at least the people working here fit the name of the place. Unlike *some* people I've met. I actually do feel a bit merry right now.

"I will," I say, and give her a smile. I instantly like Ivy. It might be because she's the only normal person I've met in this town so far.

Just as I'm about to walk away toward the other end of the counter, Ivy's eyes go wide at something that's going on behind me. Did the evil baker sneak back in while we were talking and is really going to set this place ablaze?

"Oh no. Oh gosh," she says, her voice panicked.

I turn around in time to see a little boy approach the table of men that the baker woman was referring to earlier. A.k.a. the land hogs.

"Kaden!" she yells, but the boy doesn't even turn his head toward her.

He clears his throat. "Excuse me, gentlemen?" His high-pitched little voice can be heard over all the noise, which dims when he speaks, and nearly all eyes turn toward him.

The men at the table he approached stop talking and turn their attention to the boy. He's got dark-blond hair the same shade as Ivy's—which nearly covers his eyes—and he looks to be about five, maybe six years old.

The boy stands a little taller, his shoulders going back as if he's practiced what he's about to say. He clears his throat. "For Christmas this year, I'm asking Santa for someone to be my dad. And I was wondering if any of you would like to do it?"

Ivy has come out from behind the counter and is running to the table, saying his name over and over. "I'm so sorry," she says as she nears. She picks up the boy, who wraps his little legs around her waist. She gives the men a sheepish sort of grin.

"He's just excited for Christmas," she says, giving them a breathy laugh as she pivots with the boy in her arms and walks back toward the counter.

"Not a problem," says one of them, and a round of low chuckles comes from the table as she walks away.

She goes back to the register, seating Kaden on the counter next to her, and closes her eyes like she can't handle what's going on right now.

"Kaden," she says as she opens her eyes and lasers them at the boy. "What did Mommy tell you about talking to strangers?"

"That I'm not supposed to?" He does a little pouting thing with his lips that's so adorable, I kind of want to give him a hug.

"Yes," Ivy says. "No talking to strangers. And please, for the love of all that's holy, would you please stop asking random people to be your dad?"

So this wasn't the first time, then. Should I interject with an unsolved mystery I heard last week about a kidnapping? I could scare this kid into never talking to strangers ever again. Maybe not right now.

He twists his little lips to the side, his eyes downcast. "But Santa said that he can't just bring me a dad—I have to find him."

Ivy closes her eyes and then pulls Kaden into a hug. She leans her head on top of his. "If we're meant to bring someone into our family, we will do it together, okay?"

"Okay," he says.

She pulls out of the hug and places her hands on both sides of his face. She looks him in the eyes. "Can it be just you and me for now? Can that be okay?"

Kaden gives her a nod. A sad one, with his lips now pulled into a frown and his eyes crestfallen.

The bells on the door jingle, and all three of us look over to see a man with dark hair and black-rimmed glasses walk in.

"Pete," Ivy practically cries out his name at the same time as Kaden yells it with glee. Both of their faces lighten significantly.

"Thank heavens you're here," says Ivy. "Can you take Kaden?"

"Of course," the man says, giving Ivy a bright smile as he comes over to the counter. He's got eyes that sparkle when he looks at Ivy. The kind of look that only a smitten man will give a woman.

The look is fleeting, and then his attention turns to Kaden, who smiles big and slides himself across the counter, jumping into the man's arms. They walk away over to the other side of the store where the tables are and take a seat.

I look back to see Ivy watching them walk away. She brings a hand up and puts it on her chest as if to anchor herself. "That kid," she says on a sigh.

"He's a cute one," I say.

"Thanks." She gives me a little smile. "His dad died a little over two years ago." Her eyes travel over to the plaque that hangs by the front door. It doesn't take a rocket scientist to put two and two together.

"I'm . . . so sorry."

She holds out a hand to stop me, shaking her head as if to say, *It's okay*. She must get a lot of sorrys.

Ivy shakes her head. "I don't know what to do with him. He's gotten it in his head that he wants a dad for Christmas, and then that stupid Santa in Missoula tells him he needed to keep his eye out for someone." She lets out a breath, looking over at her son. "I can't find a husband in three weeks. I don't even know if I want another one." She chuckles and gives me a sad smile. "I'm sorry—you don't need to hear . . . I . . ." She looks down at the end of the counter. "Your drink should be ready soon."

"Sounds good," I say, giving her a reassuring smile. I wouldn't mind hearing more of what she had to say but also feel like I'm prying since we don't know each other.

I walk to the end of the counter and let my gaze travel over to Kaden and the man Ivy had called Pete, who seemed to come in just in time to save the day. He's got Kaden sitting on the table in front of him and has just bopped him on the nose, which makes Kaden laugh like it's the funniest thing that's ever happened.

My heart does a little twisting thing. How sad for Ivy . . . how sad for Kaden. To lose his dad like that and want a new one so badly. Makes me realize that my broken family isn't so terrible. At least we're all here.

Watching Kaden with Pete makes me remember one of the story lines Cami mentioned last night. I pull my phone out and open my text app.

> **Me:** What was the story line about the kid and the single parent?

> **Cami:** Kids playing matchmaker for single parents

> **Me:** You can check that one off our list

> **Cami:** Are you serious?

> **Me:** Yes. I'm at this coffee shop and I just met a kid whose dad died and he's been wishing for a new one for Christmas.

> **Cami:** That's the saddest thing ever!

> **Me:** It is!

> **Cami:** Wow. Okay, so it's official. You really are in a Hallmark town.

"Drink for Mayra?" The teenager behind the counter says as she holds up my cup, her eyebrows pulled inward like she's concentrating. Apparently, even in this strange Christmas town, people who work in coffee shops will still pronounce my name wrong. Just like home.

"Thank you," I say, taking the cup and not correcting her. I never correct anyone at home either. Even though I visit the Starbucks by my office daily.

I turn to go find a seat, looking for a place strategically near my competition sitting in the corner. There's an open table between them and a man sitting by himself, staring off into the distance, with a cup of coffee in front of him. Seems like as good of a spot as any.

"You again?" a voice says before I even take a step. I turn to see Noel standing there, a smile on his face and a stack of boxes in his arms.

"Hey there," I say, returning the smile.

"Mara, right?"

"That's me." I look up at the tall ceilings and then back at him. "And no mistletoe this time."

He chuckles and then turns to set the boxes down on the counter. "Missed opportunity," he says when he turns back to me.

"They really need to add more to this place. It's severely lacking in mistletoe."

We smile at each other. I notice that Noel has nice teeth. Bright and white.

"So, what brings you into the coffee shop today?"

I hold up my cup and give him a side smile. "Um . . . coffee."

He shakes his head like he just asked me the dumbest question in the world. "Of course," he says, reaching up and rubbing the back of his neck. "Because that's what people come to a coffee shop for."

"Typically, yes."

"What do you think?" he asks.

"Of the coffee?"

"Well, yeah. But also, the store."

"It's . . . really great. All of it." I'm not just saying this. The latte might be one of the best I've ever had. "It's more like something I'd find back at home."

"That's what I was going for." He's got a look of pride on his face.

BECKY MONSON

I cock my head to the side. "Did you help do the build-out?"

He dips his chin once. "Yeah, I did a lot of the work. Designed it myself."

"You design?"

He shakes his head. "Not really; I just dabble."

"Well, the place looks great. I'm sure the owners were really happy with it."

He scrunches his brow. "Yes . . . I *was* happy with it."

My mouth drops open on its own. "You . . . you're the owner?"

"I am," he says, that proud look on his face again.

"I . . . you . . ." I point to the boxes and toward the door as I stumble over my words. "I'm sorry—I thought you were like the town handyman or something."

"Oh yeah." He reaches up and rubs the back of his neck again. "I can see how you'd think that. I guess I sort of do that too—the handyman stuff."

"A jack-of-all-trades?"

He chuckles. "Not really."

I can tell by the pinking of his cheeks that he's probably one of those people who's good at everything they do. I normally hate those people, but on Noel, it seems kind of fitting.

"How long have you owned the place?" I ask.

"Just a couple of years. I was working in Billings before I moved back home."

"What were you doing in Billings?"

"I . . . uh . . . was working for a law firm actually," he says.

"You . . . you're a lawyer?"

He gives me one incline of his head to confirm.

I angle my head to give him my best questioning stare. "Wait, so you left a law firm to open a coffee shop here, in this tiny town."

"I mean, there's more to the story. But yeah, that's basically what happened. And just as tourism dropped off, even. Good timing on my part." He does a little self-deprecating chuckle.

"Are you serious?"

He gives me a concerned look, like maybe I didn't understand. "Yes . . . is there something wrong with that?"

I close my eyes and let out a breath. "This is the strangest town I've ever been in."

"We're definitely quirky," he says.

I eye him again. "You're not also a prince in disguise, are you?"

Noel looks at me like I have two heads.

"Yeah, never mind," I say, shaking my one head.

The corner of Noel's mouth turns downward as he looks over in the direction of the tables. I follow his gaze to the lone man still staring off into space. He's got a full head of salt-and-pepper hair that matches his thick mustache, a pair of wire-rimmed glasses perched on his nose.

"I need to go talk to someone," Noel says. "It was good to see you again, Mara."

"You too," I say as I lift my paper coffee cup toward him, like a one-man cheer.

I need to go talk to someone myself. Cami is never going to believe this.

Chapter Four

"I HATE THIS TOWN!" I scream out into the oblivion where no one can hear me because there's not a person, or a house, or even a real road in sight.

I'm stuck in the mud. Well, not me, but the stupid wind-up toy car that the rental company gave me.

Yesterday, after leaving the coffee shop, I went back to the inn where I worked for a while and then watched a couple of episodes of *Cosmetics and Crimes*. Then somehow, while going downstairs for a cup of apple cider, I was coerced into playing gin rummy with Irene and Hattie. Which turned out to be a spark of brilliance on my part because the sisters, it would seem, know everything about this town.

"Noel's a Holiday," Hattie had said as she placed a trio of tens down in front of her.

This was after I subtly brought him up—and by subtle, I mean I just said, "Tell me about Noel." The sisters were happy to oblige.

"So is Ivy," said Irene.

"Used to be," interjected Hattie. "She's a Mitchell now."

"There's also Merry, Grace, and Gabriel," said Irene. "Five kids in the Holiday family. Parents are Christopher and Veronica. They're like royalty around here."

"Carole Cove royalty," echoes Hattie.

And all with Christmas names. But I guess with the last name Holiday, you kind of have to.

"What happened to Ivy's husband?" I asked, placing a five card down on the run in front of Irene.

"Oh, Kyle—he was a dear. Died in a car accident," said Hattie, a sad look on her face.

"Yes, that was hard for the whole town. He grew up here, you know. Was best friends with Noel," Irene said.

I felt a little pang of something for Noel, which was ridiculous since I hardly even knew him. It would be awful to lose your best friend. I can't imagine a life without Cami in it.

"Kyle'd be very upset about what's happening to the town," said Irene. "He was very much an advocate to keep things the way they are. Wanted to run for mayor when Chris retired."

"Shame they have to sell the land," Hattie said.

Then they just started giving me information about the land. A lot of it I already knew, like how the town was suffering from a lack of tourism and that most of the interested buyers wanted to bring in corporations that would change the whole place. I wanted to tell them that wasn't my dad's plan and that I could actually help the town but decided now wouldn't be the best time to inform them I had been lying all along.

The juiciest piece of info was that one of the interested parties was a man named David Bersham, the wealthiest resident of Carole Cove. But David and the mayor—

Christopher Holiday—had bad blood between them. Something about some bad land deal David had gotten Christopher. Christopher also didn't like David's ideas for the land. Said they wouldn't do the town any good.

Now I knew more about my competition at the auction. It wouldn't be hard to dig up some information on him and see what I was up against.

"Oh, I just hate those real estate people, coming in to change our town," Irene had said.

"I know," said Hattie, looking at her cards and then the ones we'd all laid out. "Even David Bersham, one of our own."

"He's the worst one." Irene said. "Resident who wants to ruin his own town."

"Well, I tell you what, none of them are staying in our inn," said Irene, with a very defiant dip of her chin. "One tried to book a room this morning." She looked to me, giving me a sad nod.

The room was suddenly hot. I felt like I was giving off a vibe. Do real estate agents have a particular pheromone that reveals their true identity? Two more days, I told myself. I could do this.

This morning, after getting ready and having a quick breakfast at the inn, I decided to check out the property and take some pictures for Michael, the attorney who's helping me with the auction. He'd asked me to do it when I got here since he hadn't wanted to make the two-hour drive to do it himself. The property was sort of amazing, with some of it up against the lake and the rest just a massive grove of trees. I wondered what my dad planned to do. From the sound of it, not much, other than to sit on it for a while and let it grow in value. That was what I had figured, at least.

Still, it was gorgeous land, and it had just been sitting here all this time. It was kind of a waste. The town could put a hotel on it, or little cottages to rent out as romantic getaways.

I got the pictures and was on my way back, but then decided to take a detour down a dirt road toward a little dilapidated barn I saw on my drive. Something about it caught my eye and I knew Cami would love a picture of it, since she's a photographer.

But then on my way back from the barn, I nearly hit a deer that appeared out of nowhere, which caused me to swerve and land in a ditch full of mud. And now I'm stuck. I've tried just about everything I can do. Now I have to walk back to town, which is at least a couple of miles away, since I don't really have anyone to call and I doubt you can catch an Uber around here. Hopefully they at least have tow trucks in this stupid place.

At least I was smart enough to put on my Hunter boots and my favorite black puffer jacket so I won't freeze to death as I make my way back. I've also got my Heathen Steven scarf on, of course. I tend to be an over-packer. I also have a coat problem, although I'll never fully admit that to Cami, who has accused me of it for years. In situations like this, I'm grateful for my tendency to bring too much stuff on a trip.

I'm not, however, grateful that I left my earphones back at the inn. I don't even have unsolved crimes to keep me company as I head back to the town.

I start walking down the road, looking back at my car just once before it was out of my sight, and wishing that I'd been smarter than thinking that teeny thing would make it on a dirt road. I'm grateful I didn't actually hit that deer, though. That car would have folded up like an accordion.

My phone dings as I walk, and I pull it out of my pocket and see a text.

Don't Answer This Number: Hey

Ah yes, my weekly text from Heathen Steven. A lovely addition to this stupid day. I recently changed his name in my phone to remind me to not keep going back to that idiot. It's taken me a while to get there.

Don't Answer This Number: I want to see you

I stop on the road and pull a glove off with my mouth, letting it dangle in my teeth as I text back.

Me: Wrong number

Don't Answer This Number: Come on, Mara

Me: Who's Mara?

Don't Answer This Number: Your dad told me you were out of town. Can I see you when you get back? I miss you.

He misses me? Oh please. He's fed me this line so many times it's laughable. Also laughable is the fact that it's worked in the past. But not anymore. Who cares that he looks like Channing Tatum. It no longer affects me.

I can't believe my dad is talking to him about me. I need to have words with my father. It should have been a warning bell when my dad approved of Steven in the first place.

Me: Wrong number

I put the phone back in my pocket, put my glove on, and continue my walk toward the town. I hear another ding but decide to ignore it.

Heathen Steven was all wrong for me; I know this. I just wish he wasn't so good looking. And before I get judged for being shallow, he's also funny, and quite charming when he wants to be. He's also a lying, cheating scumbag. Cami warned me multiple times. Even so, I kept going back to him. I finally stopped telling her about him because I knew she didn't approve.

It was sometime around a month ago, when I caught him texting another woman *while* we were on a date, that I finally saw the light. And believe me, I should have seen it long before. It's like I did but I didn't want to admit it to myself. I just kept hoping . . . hoping he'd be the guy I needed. That he'd come around.

But he didn't, and I have a hunter-green scarf currently around my neck to prove it. I'm growing fond of this scarf. It's a good reminder of mistakes old Mara used to make. I'm new Mara now. New and improved.

Just as new and improved — and partially freezing — me has been walking for about ten minutes, I finally see signs of civilization. A black truck is coming my way, and I wonder if I should wave and see if I can hitch a ride, because my nose feels like it might freeze off. But my extensive knowledge of unsolved murders keeps me from doing it. There are so many places to bury my body around here, and I'm just not in the mood to deal with a serial killer today.

But as it gets closer, the truck slows down and then comes to a complete stop next to me. Do I make a run for it? Before I can think of what to do, the driver's-side window rolls down and Noel's head pops out.

"What are you doing out here?" he asks, visible puffs of air coming from his mouth.

"Noel!" I say, my voice gleeful. I absolutely know this whole scenario — I get stuck in the mud and Noel just happens to drive by—is straight out of a holiday movie. Maybe I'm just manifesting it all now. Like the universe is conspiring *for* me rather than against me. The title would be *Mara Rents a Piece-of-Crap Car for Christmas.*

"My car is stuck," I say, hitching a gloved thumb over my shoulder in the direction of my stupid rental.

"Hop in," he says. "Let's go check it out."

I cock my head to the side. "You really are a prince, aren't you?"

"Nope, just a guy with a big truck."

I walk around to the passenger side. He wasn't exaggerating about this vehicle, as I have to nearly hoist myself into my seat, it's so high off the ground. The first thing I notice as I get settled and put on my seat belt is that spicy scent from his cologne. Or maybe it's his aftershave. Whatever it is, I like it.

"What are you doing all the way over here?" Noel asks as I buckle myself in and he starts driving.

"I just went for a drive. Oh, it's over there," I say as we approach the dirt road and I see my car about twenty feet away, tilting a little to the side in the ditch.

"I don't have anything to tow it with," Noel says as he turns onto the road and we pull up next to the tiny blue car.

"Is there a tow truck in town?" I ask.

"Of course. We're not savages."

"Are you sure?" I tease. "I mean, there's not even a Target nearby."

Noel puts his hand to his heart. "The horror."

"It is to me," I say. I'm not even exaggerating here. A girl needs Target. It's a fact.

He gives me a smile and then puts the truck in reverse since there's no place for him to turn this thing around on this one-lane dirt road.

"I'll take you back to town and then send Jake back out to get your car."

"Jake, the tow truck guy?"

"The only one," he says. "He also plows the streets when it snows, and he's the resident plumber."

"Oh wow. And here I thought you were single-handedly taking care of the town. Looks like he's got you beat."

"We couldn't survive without him."

I smile at him. "Well, thanks for saving me, and for not being a serial killer," I say.

He barks out a laugh. "Serial killer?"

"Sorry," I chuckle at how stupid that all came out. "I listen to a lot of unsolved murder podcasts."

"You do?"

"Yes, I find it . . . entertaining."

"Listening to how people are killed?"

"Not that," I say on a laugh. "All the investigation behind it. All the witnesses and the clues. It's fascinating."

"What do you do for work?" he asks as he pulls onto the paved road and heads toward Main Street.

I should have seen that question coming. "I work for my dad. Office manager for his company." Not a total lie. That's the job I'll have if this auction goes well. My own office to manage, finally. Just like Ben. I know what my dad said, but it still feels like I've had to work much harder for it than Ben ever did.

"I think you missed your calling," he says. "You should have been a private investigator or something."

"Nah." I wave the notion away with my hand. "I get queasy at the sight of blood."

Noel's warm laugh moves through the cab of the truck as we approach Main Street, and he turns right and finds a parking spot in front of the Mistletoe Bed and Breakfast.

"Thanks for the ride," I say, looking over at Noel as he puts the truck in park.

With a chin lift toward the inn, he asks, "How are you liking the ostrich room?"

"It's got a great view," I say. "You did well."

"I thought you'd like that."

My hand moves toward the door handle so I can get out, but I don't feel like leaving this truck just yet. This is the fourth time I've been around Noel, and it's strange how comfortable I am in his presence. Like I've known him for so much longer. He just has that air about him. A nice guy. I've never been into nice guys; I've always been attracted to the edgy ones. The ones who cause my rage crocheting. I should find me a nice guy when I get back home.

"Where's a good place for lunch?" I ask, realizing that it's been a while since I ate anything and I'm pretty hungry.

Noel looks at me. "I'd say the Jolly Café. It's right there." He points to a little storefront just a few doors down from where we've parked.

"Great," I say.

"They make a mean burger," he says. "Best one I've had."

"That sounds perfect." I'm not just saying that. My mouth waters a little at the thought. I'll pick up some takeout and head back to the inn.

I grab the handle of the door to open it again. I'm really going to exit this truck now.

"Want some company?" Noel asks just as I start to get out of his massive truck.

I turn back around.

The apples of his cheeks are a little pink, and it's nice and toasty in the cab, which means it's not from the cold.

"I mean," he says, "if you want. We could call Jake and get that all squared away while we wait for our food."

Oh, right. Jake and my car. I almost forgot about that, all cozy and warm in Noel's truck. I still have a piece-of-tin car stuck in some mud down the road.

"Okay, sure," I say, even though I have things I should be doing back at the inn. I have work I need to do, and I need to send the pictures I just took to Michael. But lunch with Noel sounds a lot less boring.

"Okay, then," Noel echoes.

We hop out of the truck and walk toward Main Street to the Jolly Café.

The outside looks a lot like the other buildings, but with a sign with the café's name just above the door. We go inside and it looks just as I'd expected. Christmas everywhere, with red and green balls attached to garland suspended from the ceiling, and more large, red and green ornaments hanging solo from the ceiling by fishing wire. There's counter seating as you walk in and red and green pleather booths lining the walls, while tables fill the center of the room. Over-the-top decorated trees are in every possible corner, with small ones serving as table décor. A low rumble emanates from the few tables. A lone man sits at the counter drinking a cup of coffee, an empty plate resting before him.

"Well, if it isn't Noel Holiday," says a woman when we enter. She's wearing black jeans and a Christmas sweatshirt.

She's got a Santa hat on her head and a pair of spectacles dangling from a cord around her neck. She's got one of those voices, low and raspy, like she's been smoking two packs a day most of her life.

"Hello, Sammy," Noel says, giving her a warm smile.

"Who do we have here?" she asks, her wrinkled eyes on me.

"Mara," I say, giving her a smile and a little wave.

"Welcome," she says, and then she just stands there. This is the part where Sammy should say "Table for two," I believe. Or maybe we seat ourselves? But Noel isn't moving—he seems to be waiting on her. She just keeps looking at us like she's expecting something.

"Can we get a table?" Noel finally asks.

"Of course," she says. "But first . . . ," she trails off as her eyes go toward the ceiling.

It can't be. But as my eyes follow hers, I can see that yes, we're once again standing under mistletoe. It's nestled between some of the garland hanging from the ceiling.

"So we meet again," I say with a chuckle. Honestly, this is getting a little ridiculous.

"Sorry," Noel says, as if he had anything to do with it.

"I think it's my turn this time." And just like we've been doing this for ages, because we kind of have—or for the last couple of days at least—I turn my head up toward Noel's cheek and kiss him. It's a quick little light one, and his cheek feels soft under my lips. Even with that little bit of scruff, that he seems to always have, tickling me. I think when I get back home to Carson City, I'll keep my eyes out for a nice guy with a little scruff too.

Satisfied, Sammy takes us to one of the pleather booths in the back corner. She hands us our menus after we settle in. We spend the next couple of minutes deciding what to eat; I pick a burger, of course. I'm curious if it's actually good or if this is just the only place in town that serves one.

Noel scoffs when I tell him this. "The Chimney Stack down the street serves them too," he says. "Besides, I'm from the big city, remember? Well, as big as they can get in Montana."

They don't have a lot of big cities in this state. In the research I did before coming, I found Billings has the largest population in the state, at one hundred thousand residents, and even that isn't really considered a large city comparatively.

"But they do have a Target," I say.

"They do." Noel nods his head.

Sammy comes over to the table with a couple of glasses of water and then takes our order. I add a chocolate shake to mine because it just feels like something I should have with a burger while in this café.

After we order, Noel calls Jake and sets up my rental car being towed back to the inn, which Jake says he should be able to do later this afternoon.

"So why were you driving out that way today?" I ask after Noel hangs up with Jake.

"I was just running home to grab something I forgot," he says.

I pull my eyebrows inward. "Where do you live?" I couldn't see any signs of life as I drove around this morning.

"I own some property not far from where you got stuck. I'm building a house." He gives me a little smile.

"Nice," I say. I feel the questions start accumulating in my brain—the real estate ones I usually ask. Like, how big is the lot? What's the square footage of the house? What were the results of the percolation test? What about utilities? But of course, I can't ask any of those things.

"Yeah, I've been working on it for a while. It's a slow process. I'm trying to do the bulk of it myself but will hire out the things I can't do."

And the questions keep on coming. *Shut up, brain.*

"So it won't be like the other houses I've seen around here?" Most are bungalow-style, some made from logs, with a few bigger homes sprinkled in.

"That's the plan," he says. "I've got a more modern style in mind. But it will still fit in with the surroundings."

"How long have you been working on it?"

"Since I moved back."

"Two years?"

His eyebrows move up his forehead. "Did I tell you that?"

"You did. Yesterday," I say. "Well, you actually said you moved back a couple of years ago, but that usually means two." I give him a little smirk.

I like remembering little facts about people. It comes in handy with work. I've come to find that people like it when you remember the small details about them. It means you were listening.

He rolls his lips inward, pulling them between his teeth. "It's been quite the undertaking."

"Big house, then?" I ask, not able to help myself. Average time to build a house is around seven to eight months where I come from. Two years will get you a mansion—like the ones my parents built.

"I mean, not huge or anything, but good sized. It should be further along than it is, but life gets in the way."

"So where do you live, then? While you're building?"

"There's a little bungalow on the property I'm living in right now. I'll either tear it down or keep it as a guesthouse or something when I'm done."

Don't ask about zoning, Mara. Do not.

"What brought you to Carole Cove?" Noel asks.

"I just needed a break," I say. This isn't an outright lie. I did need a break from home, from my mess of a family. In fact, when my dad asked me to do this for him, I jumped at the chance to escape from everything, even if it was only for a few days. It didn't feel like an escape once I got here, with Christmas being thrown in my face like it was. But today sort of feels like one. Maybe the initial shock of the town has worn off some. Or it could be because of my current company.

"What did you need a break from?"

That's a loaded question. A family that's falling apart, an ex-boyfriend who I keep stupidly going back to. Although, that's one thing I can say about this trip. Before his text earlier, I'd hardly thought of Heathen Steven today.

Because I don't want to get into all of it, I just say, "Just a lot going on back home."

Noel seems to get the hint. "How are you liking our little town?"

"Well . . ." I look around the room and then back at Noel. "It's a lot of Christmas."

He laughs. "That's kind of our thing."

"Right," I say. "I just wasn't expecting all this."

"And all the mistletoe."

It's my turn to laugh. "That too."

He laughs even harder. "Yeah, that's been a new one for me this year. Not the mistletoe—we've always had that. But the meeting up under it with someone—and the same someone too."

"I can't say that's happened to me either."

The words are on the tip of my tongue. I want to tell him that it almost feels like a setup, like someone is behind the scenes making it all happen. Well, whoever is directing this holiday movie needs to cut it out because I'm leaving the day after tomorrow. In fact, my only role in this Christmas film—if it actually is one—is to save this town from the big bad corporation, and then go back to my life in Carson City.

Chapter Five

"I'm not planning on moving back into the master anytime soon," my mom says over the phone.

This cheesy Christmas movie has hit a dramatic scene with this conversation that I don't need to be having right now.

Today's auction day and I still have some work to do, not to mention I need to meet up with Michael—who's driving up from Missoula—an hour or so beforehand to go over all the title work he's done. The good news is Michael found out he has a connection with someone who works with the county Carole Cove belongs to and was able to do some fishing around. He thinks we have this one in the bag. Still, I need to be done, papers in hand, before I can breathe easier.

"I understand that," I say to my mom. I'm not just placating her. I do get why she wants to stay where she's at. My dad, despite how much I love him, can be a real jerk sometimes. Especially when it comes to my mom. And my mom is a wonderful person and honestly deserves better. But her finding something better means our already mostly broken family will be permanently broken. I'm not sure I'm ready to accept that.

Why couldn't I have been born into a family like Cami's? She has five brothers and two parents who love each other, and they all get along. We've spent a lot of time with them over the years because our dads were business partners—Jenkins & Scott Realty—until just last month. But Daniel Jenkins recently decided to retire, and my dad bought him out. So now it's just Scott Realty. It sounds kind of boring now. At least he didn't change it to Scott & Son Realty, like I thought he would. Ben is the heir and I'm the spare in this family.

Cami's clan is more like what I expect a family to be. I've always watched in awe at how they just seem to love each other. Like they would always have each other's backs. Sure, they have drama, like any family, but they seem real while my family is always trying to keep up appearances—to look like the perfect family rather than attempt to be one.

I can't even picture my dad without a suit or golf attire. That's how he's always dressed. And my mom . . . well, let's just say she ended up in the ER a couple of months ago due to an electrolyte imbalance from working out too hard and not eating or drinking enough. All of this for my dad. So, Kellie Scott can be the arm candy she thinks he wants her to be. He's never let her think otherwise.

Then there's Ben. For so long we were close—at least I thought we were—and on the same page about what we wanted in life and how our parents' marriage was not on that list. But then he went and became just like my dad. Because of his choices, I now have to deal with Claudia Cann any time we're together. It's enough that she replaced Cami at our family gatherings, but her constant posting and going live on

Instagram makes it even worse. She *Cann* go far away. Like, another solar system.

"When will you be back?" my mom asks, sounding tired.

"Tomorrow late afternoon," I say.

"And why are you there?"

"Dad wants some land that just came up for sale," I say.

"Right," she says, like she's remembering, but chances are she never even knew. My parents have never been that great at communicating.

"I'll come over on Saturday and we can get lunch or something."

"Okay," she says, her voice sounding instantly lighter. "Oh, but let's go to that place where you can get the smoothies. I'm on a juice fast."

I close my eyes and shake my head, glad she can't see my reaction over the phone. She may be in the west wing of my parents' house, but my dad clearly still has a hold over her. I'd hoped she was coming to her senses after the ER visit, but I guess not.

"Mom, go eat a burger," I say.

"Oh," she says with a laugh. "I'm just trying to work off what I gained over Thanksgiving."

Oh yes, the holiday I've been trying to scrub from my brain. The holiday that ruined all other holidays. If I close my eyes, I can still picture her crying as she shoveled gobs of food into her mouth. Nope, I can't go there. I've got to keep my eye on the prize. Win this auction and get back home, and then Cami and I will be off to the Virgin Islands.

We hang up and I do some work for an hour, but after a while it starts to feel like the walls of my room are moving in closer. I don't know if it's because I'm nervous about the auction and all that's riding on it or if it's just that it's extra warm in here today. I go over to the window and open it up a crack, letting in the chilly air.

I think what I really need is a pick-me-up. So I throw on my puffer jacket and scarf, and I slip out of the inn with a quick wave at the sisters — who are thankfully checking someone else in so they can't chat — and head toward the Merry Little Coffee Shop.

It's extra cold today with the wind whipping through my hair, and my cheeks and nose feel like they're turning into ice blocks as I walk down Main Street to Noel's shop.

The aroma of coffee and the zipping and whirring sounds coming from the espresso machine instantly make me feel welcomed as I enter the store, keeping the frigid air out as the swinging door shuts behind me. I really love this little coffee shop. For me, it's been the highlight of this town.

And like a record player scratch, all my good feelings toward the shop end when I see her — the Curmudgeonly Baker — standing at the ordering station just like she was when I came in here the other day. It's déjà vu, except that this time she's got on a long red coat with a knitted cap on her head, but she's wearing the exact same facial expression: someone who's smelled something stinky. With the pursed lips, narrowed eyes, and crinkled brow.

"I'm going to hire an attorney," she says to Ivy, her bony finger pointing at her.

"I think that'd be a waste of money," Ivy says.

"Well, you all are in violation of my rights," says the baker, her voice loud enough to be heard over the espresso machine.

Ivy lets out a breath. "We aren't violating rights, and anyway, like I've said all the other times you've come in here, our baked goods are different than yours." She motions over to a display case that's on the counter featuring some sweet breads and muffins. Ivy looks noticeably less disheveled today, her dark-blond hair straight and falling right at her shoulders. The bags under her eyes are still there but less distinct.

"Oh, are they? Well, I'm just going to start offering muffins and breads, too, then," the baker says.

"I think that's a great idea. You should do that, Gladys," Ivy says, giving her what I can only assume is a fake smile. Even though it's not genuine, the smile is pretty on her.

"Fine. I will." The baker lady turns on her heels and practically stomps out the door.

Ivy's eyes follow as she leaves. If I were her, I'd probably send her off with a little hand gesture that means a whole lot.

"Well, she's a real joy," I say as I approach the counter.

"Isn't she?" Ivy says, looking relieved that she's gone.

"Why don't you just tell her off?" I ask, wanting to know why anyone would put up with that.

She looks down at the cash register and then back up at me. "I don't know," she says with a shrug. "I've known her my whole life. I just keep hoping she lets it go."

"She doesn't seem like the type to just let things go." Maybe Ivy needs to learn about the art of rage crocheting. Or I could teach her how to put the baker on some offensive email lists.

She chuckles. "You're probably right."

"Kaden's not around today?" I ask, looking behind me toward the tables.

"No," she says. "He's with Pete. He's at it again, looking for a dad. Asked two complete strangers yesterday." She gives me a sad nod, rolling her lips between her teeth.

"He seems to get along with Pete," I say.

"Oh yeah, Pete's great. I'm so grateful for him."

This feels like the part in the movie where you yell at the screen, "YOU AND PETE SHOULD BE TOGETHER!" But that would be overstepping boundaries for sure. Come on, though. Hasn't it ever occurred to her? Doesn't she ever notice Pete's look of longing? Because I have, and I've only met the guy once. I so badly want to ask, but I won't. This isn't my story. I'll just have to hope that they all get a happy ending. Whatever that ends up being.

"Anyway," Ivy says on an exhale, "what can I get you?"

"I'll have another one of those caramel-and-hazelnut lattes, please," I say.

"You got it," Ivy says.

"On the house," interjects Noel, coming up to the counter from somewhere behind me. I didn't even see him when I first entered the shop. Not that I was looking. And now I'm lying to myself. *Excellent.*

"Oh, hey there." I give him a small smile. "You . . . really don't have to do that."

"I want to," he says, the corners of his mouth lifting just enough to see those two dimples pop out on his cheeks.

I'm not sure why, but my stomach is shooting off little butterflies in his presence. It might be because he looks extra handsome today in a fitted dark-green sweater and dark jeans. I look back at Ivy after I realize I've let too much time pass while I stare at her brother. I believe "gawking" is the word, and I'm currently doing it. *Lovely.* It's ridiculous because Noel is not my type, and even more relevant, I'm leaving tomorrow.

"What are you up to today?" he asks, folding his arms in front of him, and I notice how the sweater he's wearing tightens around his muscles. He's quite toned.

Stop gawking, Mara.

"Just keeping to my room, relaxing." *Also getting ready to buy some land from this town.*

"Sounds like a good day," he says.

"It's not too bad," I offer a half-truth again. It's a stressful day for sure but not the worst I've ever had in this business. I once spent the day with a super handsy couple, reminiscent of hormonal teenagers, who looked at eleven houses and hated them all, but made sure to grab a butt or passionately kiss in each one. Like it was foreplay. That was a *super* fun time.

I walk toward the other end of the counter, where a different teenager than the one who made my drink the other day is making my latte. Noel walks with me.

"How's your day been?" I ask as we stand by the counter, the espresso machine making loud hissing sounds.

"Pretty typical day for me," he says.

"Out there saving the world?"

He gives me a lift of one eyebrow in question.

"You know" — I gesture around me — "all the stuff you do around the town."

He rubs the back of his neck, his eyes looking downward, his mouth a sheepish grin. He looks back up at me. "I did do a few things today."

"Do you get paid for any of it?"

He shakes his head. "Nope."

"I should have guessed that."

"How so?" His one eyebrow lifts upward again.

"You're one of the good guys," I say.

The sheepish grin is back. "I don't know about that," he says.

"Well, take it from someone who knows a lot of dirtbags. You're not one of them." I can't imagine ever making a rage scarf for someone like Noel.

Noel has a questioning look on his face, but as he starts to say something, I hear, "Latte for Myra."

I nod my head at Noel when he directs the questioning face to the teen behind the counter and then back at me.

"That's actually one of the better attempts," I say.

I grab my cup and stand in front of Noel. Needing to leave, but also wanting to stay a little longer. This is probably the last time I will ever see him. Which makes my stomach feel sort of empty. I've barely spent any time with him. Yet I feel like I'm leaving someone I've known for a while. Strange.

He looks at his watch and then back at me. "Care to sit for a minute?" He gives a little head bob toward the tables.

"Yeah," I say, some happy little butterflies fluttering around in my stomach. "Sure."

He leads me over toward a table in the corner. There aren't a lot of people here today. I wonder what all my competition is doing right now. Probably some last-minute work like I've been doing. I also wonder where they've all been staying. I haven't seen anyone at the inn that looks like a "land hog."

One face looks familiar—that same lone man sitting at the table from my last visit here, the one with the mustache. He's got a cup of coffee sitting in front of him, and he's just staring, like he was the last time. Like he's deep in thought.

"Who's that guy?" I ask as we take a seat and I lift my chin toward the staring man.

"Longtime resident of the town. David Bersham," he says, not much inflection in his tone. I gather that he doesn't have a lot of good feelings toward this David guy, and this might be as mean as Noel can be. I've really got to find me a Noel when I get home.

"Oh, right," I say.

His eyebrows shoot up at my acknowledgment, but then they settle back down, and a knowing smile spreads across his face. "I'm assuming Irene and Hattie filled you in."

"Yes," I say on a laugh. "They made me play gin rummy and were full of info."

"What did they tell you?" He looks at me like he's curious, and maybe a little afraid.

"Just that your dad and David have some sort of feud going on."

"It's kind of a long story, but that's the gist of it. Our families have some bad blood."

"Is he in here every day?"

"Pretty much."

"And that doesn't bother you?"

He lifts his shoulders briefly. "If he wants to spend his money here, I'll take it. Besides, he doesn't cause any trouble."

"Does he just sit like that all the time? Staring off? No phone or even a book?"

"Pretty much," Noel says.

That must be a lost art or something, to be able to just sit there and think, without the distraction of a screen. I don't think I could do that. Or that I'd even want to try.

"What else did Irene and Hattie tell you?"

"Hmm." I put an index finger up to my lips as I think. They told me about Kyle, but I don't think that's something I should bring up. "They told me *all* about the Holiday family."

"Did they? And what was that?"

"Just that you were a bunch of money grubbers, trying to take over the town."

His look says he doesn't believe me for a second.

"Okay, okay," I say. "I believe their exact words were that your family is like Carole Cove royalty." I say the last part in my best British accent. Which is total crap, if I'm being honest.

Noel chuckles and then stops. "Wait," he says, his eyes doing a little crinkling thing that is very cute, I must admit. "Does that make me a prince, then?"

"I think it might," I say on a chuckle.

Noel laughs too. "What is that all about anyway? The prince thing."

"Oh"—I bat a hand through the air—"it's just this town. It's like one of those Christmas movies come to life with all the decor and just . . . everything." I want to say "all the weird people," but since that would include Noel, I decide it's best if I don't. Plus, Noel's one of the highlights of this town. "Anyway, every year there's at least one story line about a prince in disguise that plucks a small-town girl out of her life and makes her his princess."

Noel's lips purse, the spot between his brows crinkling like he's not following.

"Wait . . . have you never watched a Hallmark Christmas movie before?"

"I can't say I have," he says, reaching up and rubbing his stubbled jaw.

"*Oh, well,*" I say, my voice extra dramatic. "We're going to need to remedy that."

"We are?"

"Yes," I say emphatically. "Tonight."

"Tonight?"

"Yeah, I mean . . . if you can." I sort of do a stuttering thing over the last three words out of my mouth. It was a little presumptuous of me to just throw that out there. But it's my last night here, so it felt like a YOLO thing to do. "I leave tomorrow, so it's really the only night," I tell him.

"You're leaving tomorrow?" he asks, a look of disappointment on his face. Or maybe I'm just hoping it's disappointment. *Stop it, Mara.*

"Yeah," I say, giving him a small smile. Even though I'm ready to go, there's some part of me that's a little saddened to leave. Which is ridiculous. But this town, with all its quirkiness, may have grown on me just a little. I wouldn't mind spending a little more time here. My change of heart could be due to the man sitting across from me. Maybe I wouldn't mind spending a little more time with him. Strange that I'd think that about someone I hardly know.

"Okay, then," Noel says; his lips lift upward, those two dimples giving me a lovely show. "We better watch a prince in disguise tonight."

"Excellent. Come to the inn tonight around seven," I say and then look at my watch and realize I'll be meeting up with Michael in less than an hour. "Shoot, I've got to run." I stand up from my chair and grab the latte I've barely drunk.

"What's the rush?" Noel asks with a look of confusion.

Right. I'm supposed to be relaxing today, not in a hurry to get anywhere.

"I've got a call . . . for work," I say. "Totally forgot."

I think about where I'm going this afternoon, and my stomach drops. Not for the realization that the auction is approaching, but that Noel's dad will be there. I'd never even thought of this or put it together. What if, after seeing me at the auction, the mayor tells Noel. Then Noel will know I lied. I doubt he'd want to hang out with me then.

I might be getting ahead of myself. I've only met the mayor once, and he's never even seen Noel and me together. But still. This could be the last time I ever see Noel. This shouldn't even phase me. I hardly know him. Yet . . .

"Gotcha," Noel says, standing up too. "I'll see you tonight, then?"

"Yeah," I say, hoping that will be the case. "Seven o'clock. Get ready to be wildly impressed by the cinematic quality." I ooze sarcasm when I say this, and Noel gives me a grin acknowledging that he's caught on.

I step outside the coffee shop and take a big breath of the cold air. I've got to get focused. I need to get that land so I can show my dad what I'm capable of, and then I'll finally get the opportunity to run an office.

I need to get this auction over with, and then afterward—if I don't get ratted out by the mayor and possibly kicked out of this town—maybe I'll get to watch a cheesy holiday movie with Noel.

Chapter Six

Michael and I take seats in the back row of the old town building where the auction is being held, the place is in need of some serious repair. The linoleum floor is peeling in some parts, there are water stains down most of the walls, and I'd bet everything I have riding on this auction that the popcorn ceiling has asbestos. There's also a very distinct mold smell that permeates the space.

Cami will be disappointed to know that, unlike in many of the Christmas movies she used to make me watch, there are no big productions being put on to save this place—that I know of, at least. Maybe this town building is one talent show away from being saved. Or . . . maybe a few talent shows. And, possibly an appearance by a celebrity to really bring in the big bucks, because this place would need *a lot* of money.

I look over at the man my dad hired to help me with everything. He's wearing a perfectly tailored black suit and a cranberry-and-gray wide-striped tie. He's got crystal-blue eyes hooded by thick, dark lashes, a full head of brown hair, and perfectly straight teeth.

I don't know Michael except for the conversations we've had over the phone. We met face-to-face for the first time today, and even if I hadn't already known, I would have been able to tell he was an attorney from a mile away. Not because he's the only person here wearing a suit so far, but because he just has that look about him—and I mean the smarmy kind, not the good kind. The kind that could schmooze his way around any hurdle, is willing to do shady things if it gets him the outcome he wants, and loves undertaking a challenge. He's 100 percent the type of man I go for. Or have in the past, at least. I've been trying to change my ways since Heathen Steven, and pretty much every other boyfriend before him.

I have a type—I know this even though I would never admit it to Cami, who's called me out on it several times. I *am* trying to fix it, though, to change my ways. It's kind of hard when there's a voice in my head right now saying, *Oh! He's pretty!*

He is pretty. But there's no doubt in my mind that if I did go for Michael, he would be a future recipient of a rage scarf. He's just that kind of guy.

Still, he's been helpful. He's done a lot of the groundwork, including all the property evaluations, the title search, and arranged the title insurance. I appreciate it all, but I won't be going out with him later to celebrate if we win, like he suggested after we met. Even if that voice in my head keeps asking me why not.

I need to keep my head in the game. I've got a lot riding on this auction. An entire office with my name on it. I picture *Mara Scott, Manager* on my door plaque and get a little thrill of excitement. Even if this is a family business and I was expected to work there when I got older, I love real estate. There's just something about finding the right place for someone. To match them with their home. I especially love helping people build a home. No matching needed when they can make all the choices themselves. If I could, I would do that exclusively.

Other people file in and take seats. This is getting real. It's almost go time. I recognize a few of the men filing in from the coffee shop the other day. There are about twelve of us here so far. It's a closed auction, meaning only interested buyers who are registered, members of the town council, and someone from the county who's there to oversee can attend. These things are usually open to the public, but under the circumstances, I'm sure they had to plan it this way so the town doesn't try to stop it. I'm a little shocked I didn't see the Not-So-Cheerful Baker out front threatening people with her looks of disdain. She would have probably scared away at least a couple of interested parties.

The mayor walks in wearing a bright-red bow tie, with two women and two men trailing behind him. They take a seat at the front, behind a long folding table that's seen better days. Just as they're all seated, the door swings open, and in comes David Bersham. He takes a seat in the first row, front and center. The room goes oddly quiet, like everyone knows the background story there. Or maybe it's because they're watching the wordless exchange happening right now between the mayor and David. There's a lot of hatred there—anyone with eyes could see it.

"Who's that guy?" Michael says, leaning toward me, his breath tickling my ear. He smells good, and I don't like this about him. I was hoping he smelled like rotten cheese. My brain is off on a tangent again, trying to tell me that this might be a bad boy I can tame. *Shut up, you.*

"David Bersham," I say.

"Right," Michael says, nodding his head. "He's probably our biggest competition, from what I was able to find out."

I let out a breath. I'm feeling all the pressure now—jittery, like I'm hopped up on caffeine. Which, given the latte I had earlier, I sort of am.

"Let's get started," Mayor Holiday says from his seat at the front. He's looking at his watch as he says this, a pen in his hand and a stack of papers in front of him.

The door swings open once again, and someone else walks in.

"Sorry I'm late," says a familiar voice. Dressed in a nicely tailored charcoal-gray suit, pressed white shirt, and tie, the scruff recently shaved off his face . . . is Noel.

"Glad you're here, son. Our town attorney," he says to the gathering of people sitting before him. There's a definite note of pride in his voice that matches the look on his face.

"Crap," I whisper, trying to sink down in my seat, hoping not to be seen.

"What's wrong?" Michael leans toward me, his brows knitting together.

"Nothing, I'm just a complete idiot, that's all," I whisper. Because seriously, how thick can I be? Of course, Noel is the town lawyer. Of freaking course. Just because he left his big job in the city and moved back here and opened a coffee shop . . . why would he stop being a lawyer? I didn't see this one coming and I really should have. "Is he looking over this way? The guy that just walked in?"

"No," Michael says. He's leaning down toward me as I continue to slouch as low as I can in this chair. "Do you know him?"

"Yes," I say, the word coming out as a hiss. "Don't draw attention to me."

I can see Noel through a thin line of sight between the people in the rows in front of me. He looks briefly around the room and then takes a seat at the end of the folding table.

"What's the story there?" Michael asks, leaning in again.

"Nothing," I say, annoyed that even in a whisper I can tell Michael is bothered that I know someone from this town and that he's a man. I think Michael and Heathen Steven might be twins separated at birth, because Steven marked his territory the moment he saw me—similar to the way Michael is reacting now. And to think I once found that kind of attention attractive. *What's wrong with me?*

"All right," the mayor says, his voice booming over the low rumble of the room. "Let's get this done."

I have no plan right now except to stay down like this and maybe to send Michael up with the bid while I army crawl out of the room. I know this probably won't work, but I can hope.

The man I'm assuming is from the county stands up. He's probably in his early fifties, with a round belly and sparse sandy-blond hair that most men would have probably shaved off by now, but I'm betting he's not ready to give up on it quite yet.

"On the docket, we've got listing number 44105948, a total of twenty acres for sale on the southeast side of the town, three quarters of it near the lake and the other quarter near the road. Starting bid for this auction is $1.3 million."

I keep my head down as I listen to the county man tell us all the details and the requirements for the bid. All of which I already know, since Michael may be smarmy but does his job well.

I risk a look up and see that somehow the line of vision between me and where Noel is sitting is no longer a sliver but a full view, and he's got his eyes directly on me.

I close my eyes briefly and then sit up straight. I'm not sure how I thought I could even get away with this. Especially if I want to win this bid, which I do. I open my eyes and look at Noel. He's still looking at me, this time with a sad, resigned smile on his face. No dimples to be seen.

My stomach drops like I'm on a roller coaster and have just gone down a steep drop. I don't know why I feel this way. I'm here on business, and after this meeting, I'll never see Noel again. I surely won't be seeing him later tonight now that he's seen me here. I guess I didn't have to worry about his dad ratting me out after all.

I might have told him tonight, though. After the movie I was going to make him watch. Cami texted me the title of a super cheesy one with a prince in disguise that she saw a few years back. Only after she teased me about my Christmas Boyfriend—her new nickname for Noel.

I would have waited until after the movie was over, but the hypothetical conversation where I'd tell Noel the truth had been running through my mind—the way I'd tell him and explain my reasoning. I'm sure by then he would know that the land had sold and that it wasn't going to someone who wanted to bring in a big company to ruin this little town. If I'd won the bid, that is. It was a good conversation, in my head.

Instead, after the disappointed smile, Noel turns his head away from me and toward the guy from the county, and I'm pretty sure it's the last interaction I'll have with him. Since I barely know him, this shouldn't be that big of a deal. So why do I feel sick about it? Because I hate that I wasn't honest with him, that's why. But if I had been, he would have written me off—grouped me with all the other land hogs in town.

"Are there any questions before we start the bidding?" the county guy says.

"I've got one," a low, deep rumble of a voice says from somewhere near the front of the room. David Bersham stands up, looking as if he's taking over the entire room with his tall frame and large shoulders stuffed into a dark-brown corduroy sport coat.

"Yes?" says the county man.

I can see David's profile as he angles his body toward the mayor. "Why don't you just sell the land to me, Chris? You know I'll do right by it."

After an awkward silence where the mayor and David stare at each other, Mayor Holiday says, "Your track record says otherwise."

"Can you please sit down, David?" the man from the county asks.

"Yes, please. Sit down," the mayor repeats, his words clipped. "We don't want you here."

David pulls something out of his pocket—a third of a sheet of paper that he's unfolded and is now holding out, waving it toward Mayor Holiday. "I've got a cashier's check for way more than what you're asking that says I can be here if I want."

"We don't need your money in this town," says the mayor.

"Gentlemen," the county man chides.

"You need money, and you know it, and I just so happen to have it," David says nonchalantly. "Let's just put this all to bed."

I'm gathering he's referring to more than the auction with that statement.

"Hey, don't we all get a chance to bid here?" a man in a plaid button-up shirt a few rows up from me says.

"Yeah," yells another man from a different part of the room.

I sort of want to chime in myself. I've got a lot riding on this auction. I also want it to happen. David Bersham is trying to ruin my dreams too. He's the bully in this story.

"I didn't come all this way for nothing," another man says, standing up from his chair.

After he stands up, a few others join in, and the room starts to grow chaotic. All too soon, everyone is talking over each other. David and the mayor are pointing and yelling at each other as their personal fight escalates.

I look at Michael, who looks back at me. We're both just sitting here, not sure what to do with ourselves.

"Is this how auctions go around here?" I ask him.

"Not any I've been to," he says.

Suddenly there's a loud whistle from the front, and like we're all in middle school, everyone stops shouting.

"Everyone, please!" yells the man from the county, and the rest of the chatter dies down to a low grumbling sound. "We will do this the civilized way, or I'll be forced to postpone."

I look again at Michael, whose eyebrows are pulled low on his forehead. Postpone? Is that a possibility? That can't happen. I've got a Virgin Islands trip to get to. And a future office manager job waiting for me.

"The civilized way would be to just sell me the land," David says, his face now red from all the shouting.

The mayor, whose face is equally red, jumps up from the chair he just sat in. "I told you, over my dead body. You'll screw this town over just to fill your own pockets."

"Gentlemen," the county man says again, his voice a reprimand.

But David ignores him. He walks up to the front so now there's just a cheap, faded plastic table between him and the mayor. "You're the one who ruined this town. And now you have the opportunity to fix it. If you'd get your head out of your ass, you'd see what's right in front of you. Because of your pride, we have to do this the hard way." He motions toward the rest of us, here for the auction.

Mayor Holiday leans in toward David so now their faces are only inches apart. "I did not ruin this town," he says, his words a staccato.

Noel stands up, looking ready to intervene, but before he can even take a step, the mayor's fist comes up and clocks David right on the side of his jaw.

Gasps fill the room and for a split second we all freeze in our spots, wondering what will happen next. But then, before anyone can do anything, David flings himself over the table, pushing the mayor over and landing on top of him. And then the room erupts. There's a lot of yelling and screaming. I'm on my feet and pretty sure I've let out a few screams myself, but it's all happening so fast, I can't make heads or tails of anything. Because they're behind the table, on the ground, I can't even tell what's going on save for the few glimpses I get. I can just see Noel and the others attempting to get them apart but having little success.

It's not until some of the other men who were here for the auction jump into the fray and help pry the two fighting men apart that they're finally separated from each other. Michael had attempted to jump in, but I held him back by the arm. No need for him to add to the chaos.

When they get them back up on their feet, both men are looking a little worse for the wear — various cuts on their faces, hair askew, shirts untucked, Mayor Holiday's bow tie missing, and the sleeve of David's blazer ripped. They're both breathing heavily, as one would expect from a couple of old men fighting. Noel has his arms around his dad, holding him in place, and David is being held back by someone who's here to bid. Bet he didn't expect to be breaking up a fight when he drove here today.

"Well," the county man says, adjusting his button-down shirt, which became twisted as he was trying to help pull David and the mayor off each other, his little poof of hair flopping around. "I think under the circumstances, I have no other recourse than to postpone."

"What?" I say out loud and at a higher pitch and volume than I intended. This can't be happening. I'm not alone in my anger — there are a bunch of other protests around the room.

The set jaw and red tone of the county man's face says he's not happy about this either. Or maybe he's not happy about what just transpired. Either way, he looks angry. With harsh movements, he grabs his phone from his pocket, and using his stubby finger, he jabs at the screen a few times. Then he looks up at us. "We'll reconvene on Saturday the twentieth," he says, finality in his tone.

I do the math — that's nine days from now. Is he serious? Some of the other people voice their opinions, but the county man doesn't respond. He only grabs his coat from the back of his chair and practically stomps out of the room.

I sit back in my chair as everyone leaves, hearing a lot of angry words from some very pissed off people. I watch as Noel escorts his banged-up dad to the exit, his hand wrapped around the mayor's arm as they leave. David walks himself out not long after, nursing a bloody lip with a folded-up handkerchief.

It's just me and Michael now; everyone else has left. We're still in our seats and I'm feeling a little shell shocked. Michael looks at me with wide eyes.

"Well," I say, slapping my palms on my knees. "That's that, then."

Michael gives me a little shake of his head. "What just happened?"

I can't help myself: a little chuckle escapes and I cover my mouth. None of this should be funny to me. I just watched two full-grown, older men have a throw down, and now not only will I have to go home with no signed deed for the land, but I'll have to come back to this freaking town for another auction on the twentieth — which is really cutting it close to my Virgin Islands trip with Cami. I really should be angry. But something about this town, something about everything that's happened on this trip makes this all seem so . . . fitting.

I look over at Michael, who's covering his mouth as well, but he's not able to stop himself at just a chuckle; he's in full-blown hysterics, with actual tears coming from his eyes.

I can't help myself — his laughter is contagious.

When we're finally able to get ourselves together, Michael looks at me, his face red and his eyes still watering. "Want to grab a drink?" he asks.

I know I should say no to him, to this guy I don't need in my life right now. I need to go back to the inn, report to my dad, pack up for my flight tomorrow, and find myself a plane ticket to come back to this stupid town again. But I'm not even surprised when I hear myself say, "Sure. Why not."

Chapter Seven

Maybe it's the cold air that hits my face as we walk out of the building, or the fact that I have to yank my Heathen Steven scarf over my face in an attempt to keep myself warm, but one of those things—or possibly both—makes me come to my senses.

"You know what?" I say, turning toward Michael, who's just shrugged on a charcoal-colored wool trench coat that only adds to his vibe. Even his coat screams sexy bad boy. If I go and get drinks with him, what happens after that? I'm trying to stay away from guys like Michael, not put myself right in their path. "I think I better go back to the inn and call my dad," I hear myself say, even as that voice in my head protests. *But look at him; he looks just like Ian Somerhalder. You idiot!*

"Come on, just one drink," he says, his thick brows pulled inward. He looks annoyed by this turn of events, and that helps fuel my decision.

"I've got a lot to do, and you've got a long drive back."

He lets out a breath. "All right, then," he says, his voice now matching his irritated look. But at least he isn't trying to push it, which I appreciate. "I guess I'll see you on the twentieth."

"I'll be here," I say.

With a quick wave of his hand, he turns toward the parking lot and his black Porsche 911, which is exactly the kind of car I'd expect Michael to drive.

I pull a black wool hat I crocheted out of my purse and put it on my head as I walk down the road toward Main Street and the inn. The town seems oddly quiet. No one probably knows what just transpired in the town center building yet. I'm sure word will spread quickly, as will the real reason I'm in this town, which is why it's a good thing I'm leaving tomorrow. I think the Curmudgeonly Baker would tie me up and stuff me in her oven if she found out. Even if I'm not the real villain in this story. That role seems to be played by David Bersham.

I look down Main Street as I approach, with Christmas covering nearly every square inch. I can't believe I have to come back here. I pull out my phone and send a text to Cami.

Me: Apparently my cheesy holiday film has a sequel

The little dots appear almost immediately.

Cami: How's that?

Me: Long story. Auction was postponed. I have to come back.

My phone starts to ring then.

"What do you mean?" she asks without a greeting.

"There was a fight at the auction," I reply.

"A fight?"

"Like, a real, actual fight between two old men. The mayor and some old rival."

"Well, that doesn't sound very Hallmark," she says.

"Yeah, we've definitely taken a more Lifetime channel turn here."

"This won't interfere with our Virgin trip, will it?"

"It better not," I say. "It shouldn't. I'll come back, get the land, and get out as soon as possible. Then we'll be relaxing on the beach with some piña coladas."

"Oh, that sounds amazing," she says, her voice wistful.

And it really does. It's giving me something to be excited about, especially as something cold and wet lands on my face and I look up to see big fat snowflakes starting to fall. The beach is definitely calling my name.

"Are you still going to see Christmas Boyfriend later?" she asks.

"Yeah . . . probably not. He was at the auction," I say, feeling that sinking sensation in my stomach again as I remember the look on his face.

"No," she says, drawing out the word. "Really? He was?"

"In a plot twist I should have seen coming, he's the town lawyer."

"Oh," Cami says, her voice indicating she should have seen it coming as well.

"I don't think he's very happy with me. I'll just say that." That sad, resigned smile. I don't think I'll forget that for a long while.

Cami sighs. "You're really ruining this Christmas movie for me."

"I know," I say on an exhale.

BECKY MONSON

"I guess it's good you're coming back tomorrow, right?" she asks.

"Yes, please. I'm ready to get out of this town."

"Unless . . . ," she starts.

"Unless what?"

"Well, usually in silly Christmas movies, the main character somehow gets stuck in the town so they can't leave."

"You shut your dirty mouth," I exclaim. My voice is loud but it doesn't carry in the falling snow. It's nearly dusk, and the place looks like a winter wonderland with the Christmas lights and the snow falling. I don't mind the scene before me. This little town really has grown on me. But that doesn't mean I want to stay here any longer than I have to.

She laughs. "I'm sure you'll be fine and home tomorrow."

"Yes. And you are hanging out with me tomorrow night," I say.

"Well . . ."

"Oh, I'm sorry," I say, exaggerating the words. "Do we have a hot date?"

"Maybe," she says. "I mean, yes. I do. I have a date tomorrow night."

I let out a breath. It was probably hard for her to say those words since she's only recently allowed love back into her life following the destruction my dear brother caused. "Right. I guess I'll have to get used to playing second fiddle now."

"Never," she says, emphatically. "You'll always be my number one. My ride or die."

"Mm-hmm," I mutter. "I better be."

We say goodbye and hang up, and I glance down the street toward the Merry Little Coffee Shop and wonder if I should go in. Just to see if Noel is there and find out how his dad is doing.

I feel anxious at the prospect. I don't really have any reason to. Except that . . . except if I saw Noel, I could explain . . . I could apologize. But what would I say? *Gee, Noel, I'm sorry about your dad and the fact that I didn't let you know I'm here to buy the land your town is selling. Can I offer you some mistletoe to make up for it?*

I blow air out of my mouth and watch as it makes a cloud in the cold air. With another glance toward the coffee shop, I pivot and head toward the inn. It's better this way. Noel won't want to see me, not after that sad smile he gave me at the town center building. No, right now he's probably telling Ivy everything that went down and painting a picture of me that's not totally accurate. But that's okay. I don't need him or anyone in this town to like me. I'll be back on the twentieth, hopefully scoring the land for my dad, and that will be that. I just wish it were over today so I could leave tomorrow and never have to think about this place again.

I'm nearly to the entrance of the inn, almost under the shelter of the awning on the front porch, when the door opens and I see him. Like I just conjured him up with my thoughts. Noel. He's got a long black wool coat over his suit.

I was so taken aback by seeing him at the auction that I didn't let my brain even register the fact that Noel looks *really* good in a suit. This coat isn't hurting the look either. The scruff is making an appearance again, like it couldn't stay away for too long. His clothes might be similar, but his vibe is the opposite of Michael's. Like Michael, Noel gives off an air of confidence, but not in a smarmy way. There's just something so warm about him. *Warm.* Yes, that's a good way to describe Noel. Like a fire crackling in the fireplace, a cup of yummy hot chocolate, and being wrapped up in the comfiest blanket.

BECKY MONSON

"Hi," I say, giving him my best I-hope-you-don't-hate-me smile.

"Hi," he says back, the corners of his lips lifting ever so slightly. No dimples in sight. A remnant of that disappointed smile from the auction. My heart falters a tiny bit.

"How's—" I say at the same time he says "Why—"

We do that awkward thing you do when you talk at the same time—an uncomfortable chuckle, the clearing of a throat. Then Noel gestures for me to talk.

"How's your dad?" I ask.

He bobs his head like he was expecting this question. "Pretty banged up," he says. "But he'll live."

"That . . . that was crazy."

"It was a long time coming," Noel says, with an almost imperceptive lift of his shoulders.

"So not a common occurrence, then?"

This time Noel's lips do curve up higher, making the dimple on his left cheek pop just a bit. "No," he says, with a quick shake of his head. "We don't have a lot of fistfights around here."

"Is anyone pressing charges?"

Noel shrugs. "I don't know. I doubt it."

"That's good," I say.

"So, you're here for the land, then," Noel says, his gloved hands going into the pockets of his coat.

I nod, slowly.

"And not here for a break," he says.

"No, I actually did need a break, so when my dad offered the opportunity to come out here for the auction, I jumped at the chance." He also gave me an offer I couldn't refuse, but no need to bring that up.

"What did you need a break from?" he asks again.

I let out a breath, watching it dance away in the cold air. "Pretty typical story," I say. "Ex-boyfriend I needed to get away from. A family that's falling apart. That kind of stuff."

"You could have told me."

"About the auction or my drama?"

He shrugs. "The auction — or both, I guess."

I let out a breath, my chest falling as I do. "I would have . . . I should have," I stutter. "What I mean is . . . Well, when I first got here, it was clear that my kind wasn't welcome in this town. And . . . I don't know. I guess I just thought it was best if no one knew. Even though . . ."

"Even though what?"

"I'm here for my dad, actually. The land is for him."

"Okay?"

"And he just wants the land — he doesn't want to do anything with it. At least not for now. He says he wants to keep it in our family."

"Oh," Noel says. "Why couldn't you have just told people that?"

"You think they would've believed me?" I ask, pulling my eyebrows down. I'm fairly confident the not-so-cheerful baker lady would have run me out of her store with a rolling pin before I got the chance to explain.

Noel gives me a knowing closed-mouth smile, his eyes moving toward the ground. "Maybe not."

"Exactly," I say.

"I would have believed you." His eyes shoot up toward mine as he says this, like he's driving home his words.

They hit me. My heart starts doing a little thumping thing, which is not expected. Noel is not my type. He's too . . . good.

My type is an Ian Somerhalder look-alike who's currently driving a Porsche to Missoula. That's the truth of it, even if I'm trying to turn over a new leaf and make a change when I get home, since what I've been doing so far—dating-wise—isn't working. I reach up and touch my scarf as a reminder.

Too good and not my type aside, I can't deny the attraction I feel to the man standing directly in front of me, a soft smile on his lips, snow gathering on his head. Maybe if we were both back in Carson City . . . maybe this would be the start of a different story. Maybe he'd be everything I never knew I wanted. Like a knight in shining armor come to show me what I've been missing all my life. But I'll never know that, will I?

Because we're not in Carson City, and this is not the beginning, but rather the end. In this Christmas movie, the city girl doesn't end up with the small-town guy. There's no happily ever after for this story.

Chapter Eight

The next morning, I'm frantically packing up last-minute things, shoving them into my already-overfull suitcase. It's usually on the journey home that I get annoyed with myself for packing so much. I realize all the things I never wore, all the wasted stuff I brought with me. This time is no different.

"You have a problem, Mara," I say out loud to myself as I have to actually sit on my suitcase in order to shut it. *When will I ever learn?*

After some maneuvering, I get the thing closed. But the supposedly unbreakable shell of this suitcase looks like it could burst at any minute. I'll just have to pray that it will make it home in one piece.

I make my way down the grand staircase toward the front room, having to do the one-step-at-a-time thing because my suitcase is so heavy. This is why I normally make a point to stay in hotels with bell service.

Maybe I should make my dad come do his own work for the rescheduled auction. Picturing him at this bed-and-breakfast, wearing a suit, his tall frame taking up so much space, is laughable. He's a Ritz-Carlton sort of guy. He'd never last here. Plus, if he comes out here for the next auction, there will be no Carson City office for me.

While he was disappointed about how the auction went, when I spoke to my dad last night, he seemed pleased there was still an opportunity to purchase the land. He was not at all concerned about the fact I'd have to come out here again. It was just expected, of course.

I can hear Irene and Hattie talking as I finally make it to the bottom step and roll my suitcase into the front room, where I find them chatting with a middle-aged couple I've previously seen a few times in the inn. I'm confident they're truly here for vacation and not covering up another motive like I was. I wonder if the sisters fought over what room they should get too.

I'm not sure of the reception I'll get this morning as I make my way over toward Hattie and Irene. They haven't noticed me yet, as they both seem to be over-animatedly talking to the couple. I'm sure word has spread, and they now know why I came to their town. I outright lied to these women, and I hope I get a chance to apologize. Especially since I'll need a place to stay when I come back. Hopefully they'll be understanding like Noel and let me stay.

"Oh yes, it was a disaster, so I heard," says Hattie as I approach.

"They had to postpone," Irene jumps in. "Both men are pretty bruised."

Well, they know about the fight, then . . . which means they also know about me. Why they're telling this couple all about it, I have no idea. I wonder how that conversation started. Regardless, they seem enraptured by the gossiping pair.

I clear my throat after a minute to let them know I'm here. Time to rip off this bandage fast. I take a breath, waiting to see what they will say.

"Mara," Hattie says my name like it's a rare jewel, something to behold. "Do you have to leave us? We're so sad to see you go." She does this little upper body sag to add emphasis to her words.

Irene bobs her head, agreeing with Hattie.

I pull my brows inward. Wait . . . they don't know? But . . . how?

"Uh . . . me too," I say, feeling taken aback by this.

"I hope you come back soon," says Irene. Walking over to the tall desk and looking around it, she finds a white envelope and hands it to me. "Your receipt."

"Thank you," I say. "I had a lovely time staying here. I'll be sure to tell my friends about it." I'm pretty confident I could get some people I know here with the promise they can live out their Hallmark movie dreams. In fact, that's how this town could bring in more tourists. It would be a brilliant marketing strategy.

Irene clasps her hands together by her heart, intertwining her fingers. "Thank you, my dear."

"You're flying out of Missoula, right?" Hattie asks as they walk me to the door.

"Yes," I say, feeling grateful I get to turn in my toy rental car and never see it again.

"Be careful on that drive," says Irene. "There's a big storm coming."

"She'll be fine," Hattie says, batting a hand at Irene. "It's not supposed to hit until later this afternoon."

I had checked the weather and was giving myself extra time to get to the airport just in case. Luckily the snow from last night didn't last too long. Just a dusting.

Irene's penciled-in brows scrunch as she scowls at Hattie. "Well, she should be careful anyway."

Hattie returns the look. "Of course she should; I'm just saying, don't scare the girl off. You can be such an over-worried, old fart sometimes."

"How dare—"

"Ladies," I say, holding out a hand, interrupting them. I'm finding it funny how my stay at this place started with them fighting, and now by the red color moving up Irene's face, appears to be ending that way too. "Thank you for everything."

This gets them to stop, at least long enough to hug me and let me walk out the door—but when I hear the little click as it shuts in place, their fight starts back up again. I laugh to myself as I head to my rental car.

I look down the street in the direction of Noel's coffee shop after I've loaded my suitcase in the trunk. Part of me wants to run over there quickly and say goodbye to Noel again. Which is silly because I already did when we were standing outside the inn last night.

"I just came by to tell you that I can't do the movie tonight," he'd said.

"You came by to tell me that?" I was surprised since I'd just assumed it wasn't going to happen after he saw me at the auction. I also found it fascinating. Noel is a much different breed of man than I'm used to. I'm not sure I knew that men like him existed before now.

"Yeah, my family needs me," he said, giving me a little smile full of . . . something. Regret, maybe? It was hard to tell.

"I'd say rain check, but . . . I won't be here for long next time. I have a trip to the Virgin Islands with my best friend, Cami, right after I return."

"I get it," he said.

We stood there, looking at each other, the snow falling around us.

"Well," he finally said on a breath. "I guess this is goodbye, then."

"I guess so," I said. "I hope . . ." I stopped myself because I didn't know what I hoped.

He pulled his hand out of his pocket and gave me a little wave. "I'll see you on the twentieth, then."

"Yes," I said, giving him the kind of smile you'd give to a stranger. Noel wasn't a stranger, but he wasn't necessarily a friend. "Acquaintance" didn't seem right either. Something between acquaintance and burgeoning friendship. There needs to be a word for that.

"Safe travels," he said.

"You too," I said, and then shook my head and rolled my eyes at my dumb response. I'd said the same thing to the ticket agent at the Reno airport on my way here when she told me to have a nice flight. "I mean, take care."

And that was that.

I don't know why I have this empty feeling in my stomach, the kind you get when you think you'll never see someone again. I'll see Noel again on the twentieth. So this isn't a forever goodbye, like it would have been if the auction had actually taken place yesterday. But a forever goodbye is coming, and maybe that's what's making me have this strange feeling.

I shake it off. It's all a little weird. I've got a life back in Carson City waiting for me, and soon Carole Cove will just be a pinpoint on the roadmap of my life. A place I'd visited a couple times.

I throw my stuff in my little wind-up car, and it's not long before I'm on the road, headed out of the town toward the airport. I've got a two-hour drive ahead of me and a bunch of crime podcasts downloaded on my phone to keep me company.

Farewell, Carole Cove. I'll see you again in eight days.

"Well, hello again, Ollie," I say to the stuffed ostrich sitting in the same spot where I'd left him—between the two big overstuffed decorative pillows on the four-poster bed of the ostrich room in the Mistletoe Bed-and-Breakfast. I say this right before I fall face-first into the down comforter he's perched on and scream.

As it turns out, the storm decided to come a bit early, and by "early" I mean within twenty minutes of my departure from Carole Cove. It moved a lot faster than was expected, causing a flash freeze on the highway, which then caused a twenty-car pileup a few miles up the road. So, after sitting in bumper-to-bumper traffic at a virtual standstill for nearly two hours, I waved the white flag, found a spot to turn around, and came back to Carole Cove. There was no way I'd make my flight, which from the heavy snowfall would predictably be canceled.

Fortunately, the sisters were thrilled to give me my room back—with no arguing—and said I could stay as long as I needed. I reassured them it would only be for one night as I planned to rebook my ticket for tomorrow. Apparently, in the couple of hours I was away, word still hadn't spread that I was one of the land hogs at the auction, and I'm grateful for it. Yet I'm still confused by how it's even possible in this small town.

I continue to lay face down on the bed, blindly searching for my purse, feeling around with my hand until I find it and retrieve my phone.

I look at it only to press on Cami's name, and then I plop back face down on the bed as I listen to it ring through my phone's speaker.

"Hello? Mara?" she says after the third ring.

"I guess you need to tell me what happens in the movie after the main character gets stuck in the town," I say, turning my face to the side so my words aren't muffled by the comforter.

"What? No!" Cami exclaims, drawing out the word.

"Yep," I say.

"Why . . . How?"

"Storm. Ice on the highway. Twenty-car pileup." I sound like a robot.

"Oh no. Are you serious?" she asks.

"Hella serious," I say. It's definitely next-level hell up in here. "You jinxed me. I blame you for this."

"This . . . is just . . . ," Cami starts, but then the line goes silent except for a strangled sort of snorting sound she makes, which seems an awful lot like she's trying not to laugh.

"Are you laughing at me?"

More silence.

"Cami?" I look at my phone to make sure the call wasn't dropped. She's still there.

Finally, I hear a little sniffle over the line. "I'm here," she says, her voice pitched higher.

Wait, is she crying? What's going on? "Cam, are you okay?"

"I . . ." She does the snort thing again.

"You *are* laughing at me!" I yell into the phone.

"No," she says and then hiccups. "I'm . . . I . . ." Now she's just outright laughing, unable to hold it in any longer.

"I hate you so much right now."

"I'm sorry," she says as she tries to calm herself. "This is all so ridiculous. You . . . you're . . ."

"I'm in hell!" I screech. With that she starts up the laughter again, and I can't help myself—I start giggling too. Then the giggling turns into laughing until I can't catch my breath, tears are running down my cheeks, and my insides feel crampy.

"Okay," Cami says, after a minute of hysterics. "Okay," she says again, and then takes a big breath.

I take one too. "So," I say. "What happens next in this stupid holiday film I'm stuck in?"

"Right," Cami says, taking another breath. "Well, when the heroine gets stuck in the town, it's so she can spend more time with the hero, of course."

"Of course." I know she can't see my eyes rolling, but I'm sure she can picture it from my tone. She knows me well. It's a twofold eye roll. Because that's so predictable, and because I pictured Noel's face when she said it.

"Well, what's Christmas Boyfriend up to?" she asks, reading my mind.

"Are you saying he's the love interest in this story?"

"He seems like the best option."

"The *only* option," I say. I guess there's Michael. But he's two hours away and thank goodness for that.

"Well, you do have another day there, might as well have some fun," she says, insinuation in her tone.

I snort out a laugh. "He's probably busy helping the town like he always is. Anyway, I think I'll thwart this movie and stay in my room and watch some *Crimes and Cosmetics*," I say.

She sighs. "You're ruining the movie again."

"That's my plan."

Well, that *was* my plan until somehow, an hour after I got off the phone with Cami, I find myself in the front room of the bed-and-breakfast. Complete with a crackling fire in the fireplace, Christmas music playing in the background, and learning to play bridge with Irene and Hattie on a square table covered with a thick waterproof mistletoe-clad tablecloth. Not exactly the romantic interlude Cami was hoping for. Still, it's helping to pass the time.

Not helping to pass the time? The snow that's been falling for the last hour. It's giving me anxiety, it's coming down so fast and thick. I'll just have to hope that Jake the snowplower/tow truck driver/plumber is able to get the roads plowed so I can get out of here tomorrow. My flight was canceled today after all, and they were able to rebook me for another flight tomorrow afternoon.

"So do you think you've got it?" Irene asks, looking at me and then down at the cards spread out on the table.

I'm pretty sure it's clear from the confused expression on my face I don't. The game sounded simple at first — the tricks and even the trumps part made sense to me — but then they started getting into the bid system and how you earn points and I started to wonder if they were just making this up as they went along.

I look at their hopeful faces, Hattie with her pink hair and snowflake-patterned blouse and Irene in her bright-blue sweatshirt with a Christmas flamingo front and center.

"I don't . . . ," I start.

"You just have to play," Hattie interrupts. "You'll figure it out as we go."

I take a breath. "Okay, then let's play."

"Oh, well, we need another player," Irene says, pushing the cards together into a stack, then expertly shuffling them.

"We can't just play with three?" I ask.

"Oh no," says Hattie. "It's a four-person game."

That information would have been useful before they started teaching me this complicated game.

"All right." I look around the room, which is empty except for the three of us.

We sit there in silence, Irene impressively shuffling and Hattie fiddling with her hair.

Are they waiting for someone to fall from the sky? Appear from thin air?

"Are we going to ask someone?" I finally say, looking back and forth between the two of them.

"I already did," says Irene. "When I went in the kitchen to get us some snacks."

She'd brought out a plate of cheese and crackers twenty minutes ago, while Hattie was teaching me bridge basics.

"Who did you call?" I think of Cami's words earlier, about how if this were a movie, then getting stuck in this town would mean more time with Noel. And I know—I just *know*—who Irene invited.

I'm just about to answer my own question, but as I open my mouth, the front door of the inn opens, and in walks a snowsuit-clad Noel. The wind whips through the entrance, filled with snowflakes, and makes the sprig of mistletoe hanging from the doorframe swing back and forth as he enters.

"Hey, ladies," he says, giving us a wave with his gloved hand as he shuts the door on the storm outside with his other one. "It's crazy out there." His cheeks and nose are both a lovely shade of red from the cold, and there's matted snow and ice on his hat.

I smile and shake my head at the welcome sight of him, and a euphoric feeling swirls in my belly when he takes off his hat and the hair on his head stands up in funny little patches. He takes off a glove and runs his fingers through it, and my hand twitches like it wants to help. *Stop it.*

"So glad you could make it, Noel," Irene says.

"Thanks for the invite." His eyes move to me. "I heard you had to come back to our little town."

"Word travels fast around here," I say.

"I told him," says Irene, clearly missing the joke. Of course she told him. She'd have told him regardless of needing a fourth person for this game.

Noel slides out of his boots and then takes off his thick winter coat and hangs it on the coatrack next to the door, revealing a tight black thermal top that shows off a very fit torso. He pulls off his snow pants to reveal a pair of charcoal fitted joggers underneath. Forget the suit and tie—I might like this look even better. It's comfortable meets sexy.

Hattie pokes me in the arm, and that's when I realize I've got my elbow on the table, chin resting in my hand, and I'm staring at the scene before me—Noel getting out of his snow clothes—like I've been on a keto diet and he's a plate of pasta. I sit up straight and swallow because I'd apparently forgotten to do that.

"All right," he says, rubbing his hands together as he walks over to the table and takes a seat across from me. "Let's play some bridge."

"You can be partners with Mara," Irene says as she starts to deal the cards.

"You should know that I don't have a clue what I'm doing," I say.

"Oh stop, you," Hattie says. "I told you—you'll figure it out as we go."

I shake my head at Noel, letting him know that I don't really believe that. He smiles, both dimples popping out to say hello. The insides of my stomach swirl again.

"Well, I'm not too shabby at this game," he says, rolling his shoulders and doing a couple of mock stretches with his arms, like he's prepping for a race. "I've got us covered." Why do I like the way he says "us"?

"We taught him how to play," Irene says to me.

"We did," agrees Hattie.

"How do you find time to learn?" I ask Noel, my tone teasing. "With all your princely duties."

"Princely duties?" Irene questions.

Noel chuckles and we look at each other, our own little inside joke. "She just thinks I do a lot around the town," he answers, but doesn't look away from me.

"He does," I say, tearing my eyes away from him to look at Irene. But then my eyes travel back to him. "He should be sainted."

"Most definitely," says Irene. "This town needs Noel."

"So, are we going to play this game, or are you two just going to keep giving each other googly eyes?" asks Hattie, looking at Noel and then me, her tone sounding half-teasing, half-irritated.

Noel chuckles and then gives me a big smile, dimples and all. Suddenly I'm not so mad I'm stuck here another day.

I'm actually pretty darn fine with it.

Chapter Nine

The next morning, I'm not feeling so fine anymore. In fact, I'm super annoyed.

"Roads are closed," Hattie says as I plop down in a chair at one of the tables in the front room. She places a small plate in front of me with two piping hot, homemade buttermilk biscuits, a small ramekin of butter, and another filled with the yummy raspberry-peach jam that the sisters apparently make themselves. My annoyance subsides a tiny amount. At least I get to enjoy this one more time.

"I heard," I say, pulling the napkin out from under my silverware and placing it on my lap.

How long until she and Irene find out I'm a land hog and all this hospitality goes away? The more time passes, the more horrible I feel that they don't know.

A foot and a half of snow. That's how much fell overnight. It's even worse in Missoula. Even if all the plows in Montana worked diligently to clear the roads, they wouldn't be able to dig this place out in time for me to catch my flight. Especially since it's still falling and showing no sign of stopping anytime soon. In one day, they've already gotten nearly the amount of snow Carson City will see all year.

I like snow. I'd even welcome this kind of blizzard if I were in my own house, curled up on my own couch, with a good book and a hot cup of coffee in my hands. But now I'm stuck in this dinky town, sitting in the front room of an overdecorated bed-and-breakfast, my undergarments in the laundry room washing machine, because while I may be an over-packer when it comes to most things, underwear is not one of them.

I called Cami first thing. I told her about playing bridge last night and Noel showing up, which she got a little overenthusiastic about. Then I told her about the roads being closed today, and after she commiserated with me, I asked, "So what happens next, oh guru of Christmas movies?"

"More time with Noel, of course," she'd said. "Like one of those montages they do in the middle of the movie, showing the couple getting to know each other—going sledding, frolicking in the snow, getting in a snowball fight. Then you both topple over in the snow and almost kiss . . ."

"I'm hanging up now," I said.

None of that's going to happen. Besides, I'd already said goodbye to Noel . . . again. It was after bridge, which the sisters completely schooled us in, despite Noel's claim to be good and me sort of grasping the concept after a bit.

He hugged me this time. Tight and warm. I made sure to put that spicy scent he wears to memory as we embraced. My heart was doing this erratic thing, beating in a rhythm like it was telling me to kiss him. *Kiss him. Thump-thump. Kiss him. Thump-thump.*

I told my heart to quit it. Noel and I live in two different worlds. And I thought I was going home to mine today, but nope—this Christmas movie just wants to continue playing out.

I sigh as I take a bite of the biscuit, its saltiness mixing with the sweetness of the jam in a very enjoyable dance on my tongue. At least I have this.

Hattie pats my arm. "Don't you worry—the storm should be done by tonight."

"You think I'll get out of here tomorrow, then?"

She does a little snort-laugh thing. "Oh, no. I don't think so, dear. Last time this happened, it took a couple of days to dig us out. And there's more snow in the forecast." She lets out a laugh like this is no big deal.

"Two days?" I feel my eyes bugging out of my head.

"Yes, I believe so. It could have been longer." She puts a finger to her chin, as if to contemplate, and I honestly don't think I want to know the answer.

I could be stuck in this town forever. Maybe my Christmas movie is actually just a remake of *Groundhog Day*.

I let my face fall into my hands. "Do either of you have any yarn and a crochet hook?"

It turns out that Hattie likes to crochet, so I spent the next few hours making a scarf with a brand of yarn I don't love in chartreuse—the only color they had two full skeins of. It's not lime green, but the color will definitely work. *Merry Christmas, Dad.*

I'm just dozing off to a *Cosmetics and Crimes* episode on YouTube about an uneducated man whose body was found in a field, his shirt pocket stuffed with two pages of hand-printed notes containing some kind of cipher code that only the FBI is aware of, when there's a knock on my door.

I sit up quickly, the skein of yarn I was working with falling to the floor, unraveling as it does. I quickly put it all back on the bed, now in a tangled mess, and answer the door.

"Hey," I say quickly, reaching up and rubbing under my eyes as I realize that it's Noel standing on the other side. He's got a smile on his face, and he's wearing that same snowsuit he had on last night, minus the boots, which I'm assuming are down by the front door.

Cami's earlier words move through my head . . . *Spend more time with Noel, of course.* And now, here he is. At my door. This movie is going to happen whether I like it or not, apparently.

"Did I wake you? I'm . . . sorry," he says, the smile on his face dropping a fraction.

"No," I quickly protest. "I was just sort of dozing off." I run a hand through my long hair, wondering what kind of mess it must look like right now. "What's up?"

"I . . ." He stops himself, and something like regret passes over his face, like he's not sure why he's here. He licks his lips. "I just wondered, since it doesn't look like you'll be getting out of here today, if you wanted to . . . uh, come with me." He points a finger toward the stairs.

He's got a very nervous sort of boyish look right now, and I find it makes him even more appealing. A redness on his defrosting cheeks and nose and a black knit beanie on his head only add to it.

"Come with you and do what?" I put a hand on my hip.

"Jake's working overtime to dig out the town, so I've got a plow attached to my truck and have been trying to help."

"Of course you have," I say, smiling at him.

He reaches up and scratches the back of his neck, the apples of his cheeks turning a little more red. "Anyway, it's not all that exciting, but—"

"I'd love to," I say, cutting in. I've been cooped up in this room for far too long.

"Really?" He looks surprised. "Okay, I brought you some of Ivy's snow pants," he says, pointing toward the stairs again, indicating where they are.

"Perfect," I say. "Just let me change into something . . . else." I look down and realize I've been standing here in thermal pants with hearts all over them and a black oversize sweatshirt that says *I Love Murder Shows and Comfy Clothes* that Cami bought me last Christmas. And there's chartreuse yarn lint everywhere. *Awesome.*

"Sounds good," Noel says. "I'll meet you downstairs."

I shut the door and then turn around and lean up against it, putting my face in my hands, laughing and shaking my head at the absurdity of everything in my life right now. I'm about to go drive around a town I'm stuck in, with a very handsome *nice* guy, in a plow truck. I could have never predicted this for myself.

I get over it fast because the alternative is to rage crochet while Ollie the ostrich stares at me with his glassy eyes. I quickly change into a pair of black leggings and a mink-colored cropped cable-knit sweater. I run a brush through my hair and put on a little lip gloss. Then I grab my Hunter boots, my black puffer jacket, and my Heathen Steven scarf and hat and leave my room.

Down the stairs, Noel is waiting for me, a pair of black snow pants in his hands.

"Noel, you dear," says Hattie, walking toward us as I'm putting on the pants. "You shoveled the walkway, didn't you?"

He dips his chin just once in acknowledgment. "Happy to help," he says.

"A prince," I say as I stand and pull the snow pants up, zipping and buttoning them afterward. A perfect fit.

Noel only shakes his head at me like I'm ridiculous.

Once I'm fully in winter garb, a white crocheted cap on my head, we walk out of the inn toward Noel's truck.

I realize as we step out the door that I haven't been outside once today. I've looked out my window a few times, but the snow has been coming down so hard, there wasn't much to see. As we walk out into the quiet winter wonderland, the afternoon dark from the overcast skies, snow still coming down but not quite as hard as it was earlier, all I can see is pristine white snow blanketing everything.

I should hate it. It's the reason I'm stuck in this town, after all. But I can't bring myself to, and that's . . . strange.

Noel opens the door for me, and I hoist myself into his big truck. He gets in the driver's side, and after buckling in, we take off, going slow down Main Street, the ice and snow crunching under the tires.

"Thanks for coming with me," he says as we pass by the coffee shop, the store dark and empty.

"Thanks for saving me, once again. I was feeling claustrophobic in there."

"What were you doing when I showed up?"

"Just watching this show called *Cosmetics and Crimes*."

"As one does," he says, his voice a tease.

"You should watch it," I say. "This woman named Zoe does a makeup tutorial while talking about gruesome murders."

"What part should I watch it for? The makeup or the murders?"

I scoff. "The makeup, of course."

He chuckles, low and deep, and it does little twisting things to my insides. I've been having all these feelings around Noel. I blame Cami for this. She's gotten in my head.

"What was with the yarn?"

"You saw that," I say. It's not like I was trying to hide it, especially with the green all over me. "I was just crocheting." Or rather, rage crocheting a hideous colored scarf for my dad for Christmas. I better not tell Noel this, though. I already sound crazy enough with the crime shows.

"Right. Something Hattie or Irene taught you?"

"No," I say, dragging out the word. "I'll have you know I've been crocheting for a while. Knitting and crocheting are not just little old lady hobbies, you ageist."

He does that chuckle again. He needs to stop it. I can feel it reverberate through me.

"Well, I'll have you know that I can knit," he says, and I look to see a tiny smirk on his lips. "So it's not just for the ladies, you sexist."

I pucker my lips, holding in my laughter at his quip. I like a guy who can keep up with me. I felt like half the jokes I made around Heathen Steven went right over his head.

"Who taught you to knit?" I ask.

He looks over at me and gives me a little upturn of his lips. "Irene," he says, quickly moving his eyes back to the road. I don't hold the laugh in this time.

Noel turns down a street that looks like Jake hasn't been able to plow yet. It's a sea of white in front of us, dotted with small, cozy homes on each side of the road; snowdrifts taller than me creep up siding and garage doors. Smoke floats out the tops of brick chimneys, making little swirling patterns in the sky. I almost don't want us to plow this untouched scene. It's like a perfect landscape drawing that we're about to take a Sharpie to.

Noel stops the truck in front of the street, and then, pulling up a remote that's sitting between us, he lowers the plow and starts slowly moving down the road, the snow pushing to the side of the street as we drive through it.

"This is . . . a lot of snow," I say.

Noel lets out a single-note laugh. "You could say that. I think we're nearing the end, though. The snow seems to be slowing down at least."

"That's good," I say.

"Want to get out of here as soon as you can?"

"Kind of," I say. "I've got work to do at home. Plus, I feel like it's a matter of time until Hattie and Irene find out that I was at the auction, and their hospitality might run out when they do."

"They won't find out," he says.

"Yes, they will. They know about the fight."

"That's because Frannie and Judy from the town council were there, and they told them."

"Exactly."

"But Frannie and Judy don't know you."

"I've met your dad . . . and you were there."

"Don't worry about my dad. The only person he was paying attention to was David Bersham."

"That's true," I say.

"So I'm the only person who knows why you're here, and I don't plan on telling anyone. Your secret is safe with me."

I look at his profile as he drives. "Why?"

He shrugs. "Because no one needs to know. I know how this town has reacted to . . . *your kind*." He looks over at me for a second with a teasing grin on his face. "And you're stuck here now, so why make it complicated?"

I let out a scoff.

"What was that for?" he asks, risking another glance toward me.

"You're . . . you . . ." I stutter over my words, holding out my gloved hand toward him. I sound like I'm mad, and I'm not. He's just so unbelievable, this man sitting next to me, plowing a road covered in snow just because he wants to.

"Are you mad at me?"

I huff out a laugh. "No, I've just never met anyone like you before."

"Well, I've never met anyone like *you* before," he says, keeping his eyes on the snow-covered road.

I shake my head. "You don't get out much, then. Come to the city — you'll find lots of people like me there."

"I lived in the city, remember? And I never met anyone like you."

"You hardly know me. Trust me, I'm not that interesting."

"I don't believe you," he says.

Little fluttering butterfly wings take flight in my belly as we continue down the street, the snow pooling on the side of the road as Noel's plow clears it.

The conversation flows between us as we continue driving, up and down the street and then moving on to the next one. He tells me about his family, though some of it I've already learned from Hattie and Irene.

His sisters Merry and Grace are both married and live in neighboring towns. Gabe—the baby of the family and Noel's only brother—was an oops baby. He is a senior at the high school and still lives at home.

"What about Ivy?" I ask him.

He's quiet for a beat. "Ivy's been through a lot."

"She told me that her husband passed away," I say. "Irene and Hattie said it was a car accident."

I look over at Noel and see him nodding, his eyes in a trance. It's quiet again in the cab of the truck, except for the sounds of the plow pushing the snow up and away from the road, and the crackle of ice underneath us.

"Kyle was my best friend," he finally says. "Actually, Pete—you've met him, right?"

"Not officially, but I've seen him at the coffee shop."

"It was me, Pete, and Kyle. We were friends clear back to our elementary school days. I feel bad now, but it took a lot longer than it should have for me to be okay with Kyle and Ivy. But you can't stop love, right?" Noel takes his eyes off the road for a second to look at me.

I give him a small smile. "When did they start dating?"

"After he finished high school and she was in college. I think there was attraction there, but they held back because of me." He takes a deep breath. "But then Kyle told her how he felt that summer after our senior year, and the rest was history."

"You miss him," I say. It's an observation more than anything. The way Noel's shoulders seem to sag, the downturn of his lips as he talks about his friend, about Kyle.

He doesn't say anything, and I let him have the moment to himself. I've never lost anyone that close to me, but I've met plenty of people who have. I've found that space—even in a small cab of a truck—rather than some clichéd words, is what most people need.

"What about your family?" he asks, changing the subject.

I blow air out of my mouth, making a raspberry noise with my lips.

"That good, huh?" He looks over at me, his lips quirked upward.

"Let's just say it's the opposite of yours."

"Go on," he says.

"Oh, let's see. Mom and Dad are currently separated. My brother Ben is on wife number two, who he cheated on wife number one with."

"Got it," Noel says.

"Your family is like *Full House*, and mine is more like *Jerry Springer*."

"I wasn't raised by my dad and two quirky uncles," Noel quips.

"You know what I mean," I say, laughing.

"No family is perfect," he says. "My dad just got in a fistfight with his archnemesis at a land auction."

"That's true," I say. "And here I thought your family was Carole Cove royalty."

Noel snorts. "And I'm a prince."

"Well, that part is accurate." I gesture toward the road that Noel is currently plowing and not getting paid for.

"Speaking of princes, you promised me a movie," he says, reminding me of our canceled plans the night of the auction.

Why does that seem like a different time? It was only two nights ago.

"So I did," I say. "I better make good on that."

"You better."

⟡⟡⟡⟡⟡⟡

"That was . . . awful," Noel says. We're sitting on a red-and-green plaid upholstered sofa that's surprisingly comfortable, campy music playing while the credits roll across the screen. Our feet are propped up on a wood coffee table, our heads resting on the back of the couch. We're in a room the sisters proudly call "the movie room" that was most likely once an office and smells of cinnamon and wood polish. The only thing that makes it a movie room is the medium-size flat-screen television. Otherwise, the place looks very much like the rest of the first floor. Christmas everywhere. There's even a Christmas tree in the corner, decorated in all things mistletoe. *Of course.*

After plowing many of the town's roads—I even gave it a try for a bit at Noel's insistence—we came back to the inn. We parked, and as we walked to the door, I grabbed a fistful of snow, packed it into a snowball, and just before going inside, threw it at Noel. Right at the back of his head. He apparently had the same idea, because I got hit by one on the shoulder. Cami will be sad to know that it didn't turn into a full-on fight, ending with us sprawled in the snow and almost kissing.

Instead, I knew I was up against a pro, so I pretended to be more hurt than I was. When Noel came over to check on me, apologizing as he did, I grabbed a bunch of snow and shoved it into his face, rubbing it around. Then I yelled "Sucker!" and ran into the inn. Noel followed me inside, snow packed into his stubble, brows, and even his eyelashes. I doubled over, my sides aching with laughter.

Irene and Hattie fed us some homemade cheesy potato soup and rolls. Then they showed us to the movie room. Using the screen mirroring function on my phone, we watched the movie Cami had told me about: *The Prince and the Waitress*. We invited Hattie and Irene to join us, but they both declined. Smart move on their part.

"You're welcome," I respond. I could have predicted he wouldn't like the movie. These kinds of flicks are generally not geared toward a male audience. The weird thing was, I didn't totally hate it. Maybe it's this town, or maybe it's the company.

"I mean, the whole subplot with the jealous woman with the terrible Swedish accent—who clearly had her sights on the prince—trying to sabotage the wedding. Then one conversation and suddenly she's a bridesmaid?" He's wearing another pair of joggers, this time in black, with a fitted long-sleeved burgundy tee that makes his blue eyes pop. His feet are resting on the coffee table, crossed at the ankles.

"Welcome to the world of holiday movies," I say, wrapping a throw blanket around me, since sitting here stagnant has made me cold.

"And how did she not know he was a prince? Or some high-level person at least. He literally had two bodyguards following him everywhere."

"Love is blind," I say, my voice purposefully wistful.

"And the prince hardly knew the waitress before he invited her to his castle," Noel keeps going.

"Well, she did give her extra change to the homeless guy when they went on that walk in the fake snow. He saw her heart," I say, putting a hand on my chest dramatically.

"Oh, right," he says, sarcastically. "That's totally grounds for a relationship."

"Wanna watch another?" I ask, giving him a double eyebrow raise. I sound like I'm joking, but I'm not really. I'd love to stay in this little room and watch another cheesy movie with Noel.

He looks at his watch, and then back at me. "As much as I'd love to do that, I better get out there and plow some more."

"You're going back out to do more?"

"Yeah," he says like he's surprised I'd think otherwise. "The sooner we get the roads done, the sooner you can leave."

"You don't know that," I say. "I've heard that Missoula got hit worse. When does the snow let up around here?"

"April, if we're lucky, but usually May."

"May?" I say, horrified.

"It's even snowed in June."

"The horror," I say, mock terror in my voice.

"We may not be able to dig your little car out until June," he feigns worry.

"I'll just ditch that crap car if that's the case. Not worth it."

Noel does that low rumble chuckling thing again, his eyes focusing up on the popcorn ceiling. I roll myself to the side, facing him, so I don't have to keep twisting my neck.

The room is quiet now that the credits have finished rolling. The screen has switched to a screen saver, scrolling through exotic and beautiful places around the world, and only the ticking of a grandfather clock in the other room can be heard. If Noel rolled to his side, toward me, then we'd be closer, our faces a few inches apart. The thought makes my heart start to do that pitter-patter thing again. *Kiss him. Thump-thump. Kiss him. Thump-thump.*

Noel does turn toward me, but just his face. "Thanks for introducing me to cheesy holiday movies," he says, one corner of his lips pulling upward.

I snort out a laugh. "I'm not sure you're really grateful."

"I am," he says. "I know what I've been missing out on, and I can avoid them on purpose now."

"It's probably for the best."

"Thanks for coming with me today," he says, his dreamy blue eyes on me.

"Thanks for entertaining me."

"In a plow truck? I really know how to sweep a woman off her feet."

"Very swoony," I say, my voice intentionally breathy and low.

He's smiling now, but then his eyes drop to my mouth and the smile falls, turning into something more serious. I feel my heartbeat start to pick up as the air between us shifts, little sparks taking flight. I swallow slowly, waiting, hoping that he'll lean in toward me. That he'll close the distance. *Kiss him. Thump-thump.*

Noel clears his throat and turns his head away, his eyes going back to the ceiling. The sparks that had begun fizzle and fall down between us in a pile of ash.

He was right to do it, to turn away. I don't live here. As soon as this weather clears up enough for me to get out, I'll be on the next flight. Even if I'm somehow stuck in Carole Cove until the auction, I'll still be leaving after I win the bid. There is a ticking time bomb on this thing between Noel and I, whatever it is. Best to keep it simple.

I'm all wrong for Noel anyway. He's just so . . . good. A saint. A country bumpkin. And I'm a city girl with a broken family.

It would never work.

Chapter Ten

The next afternoon, I'm walking down a slowly melting Main Street wrapped in my cream-colored double-breasted coat with the black buttons. Mother Nature decided that she would allow a little lift in temperature after the storm. Not enough to get out of here, of course. But at least enough for me to get out of my ostrich room, and I'm grateful. The skies are a hazy shade of blue, and the sun is sparkling off the newly fallen snow.

After breakfast at the inn, where Irene and Hattie sat with me and plied me with questions about Noel, I finished the scarf for my dad, had a quick conversation with Michael—who I hadn't heard from since turning him down for drinks after the auction—and then looked out my window and saw that there were signs of life. The street had been plowed, the sidewalks shoveled, and it looked like some of the stores were starting to open.

Why, I'm not sure, since no tourists could get into this town if they tried. Every town south of here, all the way to

Missoula and beyond, got hit with one of the worst blizzards they've seen in years, according to the news. Carole Cove actually got the least of it, with nearly two feet.

The only people here besides residents would be those held hostage by the storm like me. And as far as I know, there aren't many. There's only one other couple at the inn, who've kept to their room except when coming down for food. The only other place to stay in town is another bed-and-breakfast on the other side of Main Street (which Irene said was a disaster and has on good authority is infested with bedbugs) that could have a few customers, but essentially it's just people who live in this small town.

I take in a breath as I walk down the street, heading toward the coffee shop and hoping it's open. I need some coffee. And okay, I wouldn't mind if Noel were there. Although, I doubt he is. He was probably out there plowing until the early morning and is home now, sleeping. I feel guilty about watching a movie with him now. Had I known he'd go back out afterward, I would have told him we could watch it another time. Then maybe we could have been sneakier and the sisters wouldn't have gotten any ideas.

"So how did it go with Noel last night?" Irene had asked after she laid down a plate of fried eggs and breakfast potatoes in front of me. This was after Hattie had set down a plate with two fresh biscuits with the heavenly raspberry-peach jam. They both sat on either side of me at the table, looking at me with wide, excited eyes.

"It was fine," I said, not giving away anything. Not that there was anything to give away. I wasn't ready to share that the time I spent with Noel yesterday had been the highlight of my life over the past few months. Even if it was spent in a truck plowing snow, and then in the overdecorated pseudo- movie room of a bed-and-breakfast watching a pretty terrible movie.

I keep playing the almost kiss over and over in my head, chastising myself for not just leaning in and making it happen. Then chastising myself for that thought and reminding myself nothing can happen with Noel.

"He needs a good girl," said Hattie, tapping the table with her fingers.

Irene agreed with a single bob of her head. "No one in this town is worthy of our Noel," she said, giving me an eyebrow lift, insinuating I was. If she only knew the real reason I'm in this town. She wouldn't be saying any of this. I'd probably have no place to stay and would have frozen to death in my tin car.

Now, walking down Main Street—watching the community as they help each other remove huge icicles hanging from awnings, shovel snow for each other, and pour salt on the icy sidewalks in front of the stores—I can see why they're all so protective of their town and don't want someone coming in here and changing their simple, happy way of life.

I feel a trickle of nerves run through me as I realize I need to win this auction for reasons beyond proving to my dad I can do it and securing my own future within the family business—I also need to win it because securing this land for my dad seems to be the only way to preserve this town as it is. *The Real Estate Agent Who Saved Carole Cove* is back in production.

When I arrive at the coffee shop, at first glance it looks to be closed, and I feel disappointment sweep over me. On a whim I try the door, and it opens.

"Mara," a voice says, and I see Ivy, working on wiping down the long butcher block counter.

"Hey," I say with a little wave. "Are you . . . open?"

"For the four tourists that are still in this town?" She huffs out a laugh. "I guess we are." She gives me a bright smile. She looks well rested today, like the day off yesterday was just what she needed. She's pretty in a very classic way, like she doesn't have to work all that hard at it.

The place is mostly empty, save Kaden sitting at a two-person table, looking very serious about a coloring page in front of him, and a lone man at a table in the corner with a book and a cup of something in his hands.

"What can I get you?" she asks, setting down her rag and moving over to the ordering station.

I try something new this time, a white-chocolate-and-peppermint latte.

Ivy takes my payment, and then with a chin lift toward the end of the counter, she says, "It's a one-woman show today. I'll meet you at the other end of the counter with your drink."

I walk slowly toward the other end as she gets to work, the zipping and whirring sounds coming from the espresso machine. It feels sort of empty and cold with so few people here, like the energy is missing.

"Here you go," she says after a couple of minutes, handing me a paper cup with a lid.

"Thanks." I take the cup from her. It feels warm in my cold hands. I take a sip, and just like the moment when the prince first meets the waitress in the movie last night, I have my own version of insta-love with the combination of white chocolate and peppermint flavors. "Wow, this is so yummy."

"It's one of my favorites too."

I take another sip, the heat makes my insides feel all lovely and cozy.

"So . . . is Noel coming in today?" I feel like the appropriate amount of time has passed before I asked the question, even though it was on the tip of my tongue when I entered the shop. I have no idea how close Ivy and Noel are, so I'm attempting to play it cool, just in case he's said something about me.

No knowing grin or other tell flashes across her face. Instead, she scratches a spot on her arm, her eyes in Kaden's direction. She brings her attention back to me. "I'm not sure," she says. "I haven't even heard from him yet. He was probably out late plowing the roads."

"Right," I say, wondering if I should tell her that I helped him for a while, and was also the reason he was probably working even later. I decide not to.

"That man," she says, sounding exasperated as she makes her way back down the counter in the direction of the ordering station. I follow her because I'd like to hear what she has to say. Fortunately, she keeps going. "He never takes time for himself. Always doing stuff around this town. Everyone appreciates it, of course, but . . ." She stops, shaking her head.

"But what?" It feels weird asking, like I'm in high school, using a sibling to fish around for more info about the boy I have a crush on. This isn't high school, and I don't have a crush. Even though I keep thinking about him and wondering what he's up to and wishing I could see those blue eyes of his. Which sounds . . . a lot like a crush. I should just stop denying it. But just because I have one, doesn't mean I have to do anything about it.

She exhales loudly. "It's not his responsibility to take care of the town."

"He doesn't seem to mind doing it."

She gives me a sad smile. "No, he doesn't. But I worry that it will get to him. And this town seems to lap it up, not worrying about how taxing it could be on someone. My husband was the town fix-it guy before he died, so I know." She looks out the window of the shop, shaking her head slowly. "But at least he got paid to do it, you know?" She looks back at me. "Noel doesn't even charge anyone. He's not responsible; neither is Pete. I never asked them to come back, and yet they both did . . ."

She cuts off, her eyes snagging on something outside, her brows pulling inward.

I want to pause and rewind and make her pick up from where she left off, even if it feels like snooping into Noel's life, which I have no right doing. I'm just so curious.

I follow Ivy's line of sight toward the glass front door to see David Bersham walking toward the shop. He's got on a brown utility jacket over his signature corduroy sport coat, and duck boots on his feet. He comes up to the door, and cupping his eyes with his hand, he peers inside.

"Does he really think he can come in here?" she says.

She walks over to the door with determination, her shoulders set, and I worry that I'm about to witness another Bersham/Holiday fight. Instead, she blatantly locks the door and flicks off the *Open* sign, which is hard to see with the sunlight reflecting off the store window.

He gets the point, and with a quick dip of his head, he turns and keeps walking down the street.

"The nerve of that man," she says, coming over toward me. I'm actually surprised by this exchange, given the fact she's let the Curmudgeonly Baker come in here and basically berate her in front of everyone on the daily. But I gather this David Bersham thing has a lot more history.

"I heard about the fight," I say, even though I want to say I saw it firsthand. But I hardly know Ivy. I'll let Noel tell her I was at the auction if he wants to.

She rolls her eyes. "That feud has gone on for so long."

"What's that all about?" I ask, unable to help my curiosity.

"Oh." She bats a hand through the air. "Years ago, when our family moved to this town—I was only four at the time; Noel was two."

This makes me picture a little toddler with crystal-blue eyes, and my heart does a little tugging thing. I bet Noel was the cutest kid.

"My dad wanted to invest in the town—he's practically made it what it is today." A look of pride flashes across her face when she says this. "Anyway, David Bersham owned quite a bit of it when we first moved here and sold some to my dad. It was a bad deal. I believe it had to do with zoning."

"Oh yeah, that happens a lot." I nod my head quickly and then stop myself. "Uh . . . or so I've heard." *Good one, Mara.*

"David claimed there was no way out of the deal, and my dad lost a lot of money—it took a while for our family to get back on our feet."

"But everyone's good now?" I can imagine what a setback that would be for their family. That David Bersham is the actual Grinch.

"My mom and dad do just fine. Mom works at the elementary school as a kindergarten teacher, pretty much since we moved here, and Dad, besides being the mayor, owns quite a bit of the property on Main Street and around the town."

"Interesting," I say, holding my tongue on all the rapid-fire questions my real estate–wired brain is currently shooting off.

"It's all old news around here," Ivy says, going back behind the counter and picking up the rag she was using. "What about you?"

"Me?" I ask, pointing to myself.

"Yeah. How is being stuck here going?" She gives me a little half grin.

"It's . . ." I lift a shoulder. "Fine, I guess." The truth is, it's not terrible.

"What do you do back in . . . Wait, where are you from?" she asks.

"Carson City," I say, feeling uneasy about where this conversation is going. Next question will for sure be about work.

Before she can ask me, the bells on the door jingle as it opens and Noel walks in, keys in hand, a woman probably in her fifties following closely behind.

"Mara," he says, his voice indicating he's surprised to see me, and his sparkling eyes and the instant upward turn of his lips tell me he's happy about it.

"Hey." I give him a little wave, my insides turning to Jell-O. I missed him. I missed Noel Holiday and I just saw him last night. Oh yes, I definitely have a crush.

Ivy clears her throat purposefully, indicating she saw the exchange between us. It snaps Noel back to the present. "Why was the door locked?" he asks her, turning his full attention toward her.

"David Bersham tried to come in." She gives him wide eyes.

Noel doesn't say anything; he just lets his shoulders drop a little.

"He did not," says the woman who walked in with Noel, her voice exasperated. She looks classy standing there with her hands tucked in the pockets of her heather-gray wrap coat which ties at the waist. I'm instantly envious of her chocolate, shoulder-length locks and wispy bangs. Her glossy red lips complete her stylish look.

"Hi, Mom," Ivy says just as Kaden yells, "Nana!" and runs over to the woman, wrapping his little arms around her leg.

"Hello, my Kaden love," she says, running her fingers through his dark-blond hair. He pulls away and she leans over, hands on knees as she looks him in the eyes. "What are you doing today?"

"Coloring," he says, his eyes bright. "Wanna help?"

"Absolutely," she says, letting him take her by the hand and guiding her over to the table he was just sitting at.

I watch as she takes a seat, instantly enamored with the drawing Kaden had been doing, like it's the most perfect thing she's ever seen. Her eyes are wide and there's a smile on her face.

Ivy goes back to cleaning the counter, and Noel comes over to me.

"What time did you go to bed last night?" I ask him as I look over his tired face, keeping my voice low so no one else can hear.

He runs an index finger and thumb down his extra stubbly chin. "Around five."

"Overachiever," I quip, and he smiles.

"Come on." He tips his head toward the seating area. "Come sit with me."

Butterflies fight for space in my stomach as I follow him over to a table in the corner. I take note that the table is across the room from where Noel's mom and Kaden are sitting.

I take off my scarf before sitting down, pulling my hair over my shoulder. Noel unzips his navy-blue puffer jacket before sitting, revealing a dark gray fitted sweater underneath.

"What have you been doing this morning?" he asks.

"Oh, just living the dream," I say. "I finished a scarf for my dad"—which turned out hideous; I'm so proud of it. "I watched some *Cosmetics and Crimes* and listened to Irene and Hattie argue over where to put a wreath they made." That *did* happen, but it was a shorter fight—I'd just rather not tell Noel they spent my entire breakfast fishing around about our evening together.

"That does sound like a dream," he says, the side of his mouth pulling upward.

"I thought about rewatching *The Prince and the Waitress* but then thought you might be jealous if I watched it without you."

He laughs a real, genuine laugh. "You know I would've been." His smile drops a little as he looks at me.

"What?" I ask, wondering if I have something on my face with the way he's studying me. I reach up and trace my lips with my index finger to make sure there are no remnants of foam from my latte or something else more embarrassing, but feel nothing.

"You look really pretty this morning," he says.

The butterflies multiply. I've been told I'm pretty before. Heathen Steven told me plenty of times. It was always with a "but." *You look pretty tonight, babe, but . . .* The way Noel says it feels so real, like the most genuine compliment I've ever received. It's something about the way he looks at me, the way his gaze sweeps across my face.

"So do you," I say. I'm not just returning the compliment because he said it to me. Even tired, Noel is looking quite handsome today, that scruff on his face extra thick. My hand twitches to touch it.

"Who do we have here?" a voice says, and like we've been in some sort of trance, staring at each other, we each quickly dart our gazes up to the person standing in front of us, a curious smile on her pretty lips.

"Mom," Noel says, the apples of his cheeks turning a light shade of pink. He gestures to me. "This is Mara. She got stuck here during the snowstorm. She's staying at Irene and Hattie's place."

"Well, hello there, Mara," she says in a sweet voice, leaning down on her knees so she's eye level with me, like she did with Kaden. "I'm Veronica. I'm Noel's mom." She cocks her head to the side. "And where are you from?"

"Mom," Ivy calls over from behind the counter. "You've got kindergarten teacher face on again."

Veronica gives her daughter a shake of her head as she stands back up. "I do not," she says to Ivy.

"You totally do," Noel says.

She turns back to me with a faux exasperated look, like, *Can you believe these two?* "Sorry that my children are so disrespectful," she says to me. "I've got three others that are much better behaved."

Noel scoffs at this, making a snorting noise, which makes me wonder what the other three are like.

"Oh stop," she says to him. Her eyes turn to me again. "So where are you from?" I notice that she's standing straight this time and purposefully trying to school her facial features so they aren't quite so teacher-like. I suppose if you've been teaching kindergarten for so long, it's kind of hard to snap out of it.

"Carson City, Nevada," I say.

"And what brings you to our town?"

I give Noel a little look. "She's here for a visit, Mom," he says without a flinch. I'm grateful he said it for me so I didn't have to.

"And you got stuck here in the storm?" Her eyes widen.

"I did," I say, giving her a closed-mouth smile.

"Well, I'm sure they're taking good care of you at Irene and Hattie's place." She looks to Noel. "You should bring Mara to family dinner tonight."

"Oh, I . . . ," I start to protest, holding out a hand.

Noel looks to me. "You should come."

Veronica gives me bright eyes and then turns to Noel. "Grace and Merry didn't get as much snow as we did, so they plan on joining us."

"My other sisters," Noel informs me, even though Hattie and Irene already filled me in. "They live in a town north of here."

"Thank you, but . . . ," I start again. I feel all kinds of nerves spread through my body. I can't have dinner with Noel's family. That's just . . . I'm not . . . How could . . .

"Oh, you have to. I insist," Veronica says. She looks over toward the counter at Ivy, who's currently leaning against it, looking at her phone. "You tell Pete to come too, Ivy." Ivy gives her a thumbs-up.

"What else are you going to do tonight?" Noel asks me when I look at him, my eyes clearly telling him to help me out here. Apparently, he's siding with his mom on this one.

He's got me there, though. What would I do tonight? Probably play gin rummy with the sisters while they interrogate me about Noel.

I let out a breath. "Okay, sure," I say.

"Wonderful," Veronica says, her smile bright. "I better go. I have lots of work to do."

She leaves us and I turn to Noel. He's got a little smirk on his face. "Come on," he chides, probably after seeing my wide what-did-you-get-me-into eyes. "It'll be fun."

I shake my head at him, but I can't help the smile on my face. "It better be," I say.

Chapter Eleven

I don't have dinner with my family all that often, and the last time we were all together was Thanksgiving. And it was a disaster.

I had this idea of doing a really quaint dinner at my place, rather than the sterile dining room at my parents'. It was going to be a dinner like Cami would have with her family, minus the massive number of people she's related to. But like Cami's family, we'd all smile and talk about normal things. We'd be a *real* family.

I planned for days, thought about it for weeks. I watched videos on the ideal table setup and purchased new plates and silverware. Everything was going to be perfect.

I prepped as much as I could beforehand so I wouldn't be flustered with everything on Thanksgiving. When the day came, I felt good about all the planning because I knew it was going to be worth it and everything was going to go smoothly. I just had a feeling.

Then my family showed up.

My parents arrived first, and it was clear from the moment they stepped through the door something was wrong. My dad had that stern look on his face I've seen many times before—his set jaw, lips turned downward. My mom's red-rimmed eyes, and the fact that she made a beeline for the wine and poured herself a full glass as soon as she walked through the door, were my next warning. I didn't ask what was wrong because I was trying to make this dinner the best we'd ever had. So instead, I pushed my shoulders back, determined to make this work, and tried to lighten the room, chatting with both my parents, trying to keep them engaged in the conversation. It started to work, I think. They were both starting to respond to my questions and seemed to relax a little. Then Ben and Claudia showed up.

At first it seemed like things would go okay. I had everyone take a seat, and we all went around the table saying what we were grateful for, which was something I learned from Thanksgiving dinner with Cami's family. My mom went first, saying she was thankful for me and this dinner. My dad went next. He said he was thankful for the changes coming to the agency with Cami's dad announcing his retirement.

When it got to Claudia, I held my breath, waiting for what might come out of her mouth, but instead she said she was grateful to be able to share Thanksgiving with all of us. I felt myself softening a little toward her. I'd one million times rather it be Cami in that seat—and it should have been—but Claudia was in my life, and I figured maybe I should just start accepting it.

Then I brought out the food: turkey, mashed potatoes, stuffing, and all the other yummy side dishes I'd prepared, including homemade rolls that were melt-in-your-mouth delicious, if I said so myself.

That's when things really went south. Everyone was being very complimentary about my spread, except for Claudia, whose eyes kept widening as I presented every dish. Every once in a while, she'd lean over to Ben and whisper something in his ear that looked like a plea of sorts, and he'd just shrug her off.

We started to fill our plates—well, everyone except Claudia, who was still looking at the food with wide eyes.

Then my dad said, "Pass the potatoes, please," to my mom, and for some reason—which I still don't understand to this day—it set her off.

"Of course," she'd said, her lips pulled up into a sort of Joker-looking smile, sinister and malicious. It was a little frightening, to be honest. "Just like the pass you made at your assistant." She smiled around the table, this time showing teeth as she practically slammed the bowl of mashed potatoes in front of my dad.

"What?" I asked, looking back and forth between them. My dad just shook his head, his eyes telling me not to get involved. I knew his assistant; I'd worked with her plenty of times. I really hoped what my mom was saying wasn't true. She could be a bit overdramatic at times.

Claudia let out what I can only assume was her version of an uncomfortable laugh after the potato incident, but it sounded more like a high-pitched witch's cackle. She decided the best course of action was to glide right over that remark from my mom, and I have to say, I was actually grateful for her in that moment. Even as she asked if we minded if she did a little livestream of dinner for her fan page. She didn't wait for anyone to say yes. She pulled her phone out of her purse, pressed the live button, and started right in.

"This is Claudia Cann, and I'm here with this beautiful spread for Thanksgiving dinner." She turned the camera so you could see her and the food I'd worked so hard to prepare in the background. I was feeling a little proud of myself at this point because it did look amazing. It felt good that I was being recognized for it, live on Instagram.

"I want to talk to you about what you can do when you're at Thanksgiving dinner and there's literally nothing you can eat," she started. I let out a gasp and looked to Ben for help, my eyes telling him to please control his wife, but he was staring off into space, like he was questioning everything that had brought him to this point in his life.

"I have no healthy options here, so what can I do? Well, let me tell you. You could ask the hostess for some vegetables," she said, her face bright like this was the best idea in the world. "There are usually some raw leftover carrots or celery that were used for the stuffing. You could ask if they have any salad options. Also, before you dig into the turkey, make sure you know how they prepped it. Many recipes cover the bird in heaps of butter, so be sure to ask before you eat it! And if you do, make sure you only eat white meat. It has the least amount of fat. Most importantly, you remember those goals you've set, and don't let them slide, even during the holidays. And don't forget, if Claudia Cann, you can too. Toodles!" She smiled into the camera, delivering the signature line she says on every video, before ending the livestream.

She gave Ben another wide-eyed glare before turning on me. "I suppose Ben didn't tell you that I require a low-fat meal for Thanksgiving."

"Um . . . no," I said.

"Well, then do you have any celery or raw carrots?" she asked, her eyes doing this blinking thing I had never seen her do before this moment. Like the twitching habits of a psycho.

I just stared at her, realizing that she and I would never be friends. I'd never be able to accept how badly Ben had ruined everything with Cami — who was, by far, the best person in the world and someone he never deserved. He had been a better version of himself with Cami, at least up until the part where he ruined their marriage. Claudia was the personification of everything that was wrong with my brother. Selfish, thoughtless, arrogant.

I really wanted to tell Claudia where she could shove her celery, but I held my tongue because I'd worked so hard on this meal, and damnit, we were going to get through it without me throwing stuffing in her face, even if my hand was itching to do so.

"Well," said my mom, and I thought she would defend me, maybe put Claudia in her place. Instead, she turned to my dad and said, "Claudia requires a low-fat meal, and I require a husband who doesn't sleep around with every female he comes in contact with."

"I didn't sleep with her," my dad's voice rang through my small apartment.

After this outburst, both couples started fighting. Claudia telling Ben that he never listens to her. My dad reiterating to my mom that he didn't cheat on her and this was not the place to bring it up. My mom telling him he's always been a cheater and crying while piling mashed potatoes on her plate and then shoveling them in her mouth.

I just sat there feeling defeated, watching the chaos all around me, wishing I could be anywhere but there. It ended with my dad storming out of my place, Claudia and Ben not far behind. I had to drive my mom home later, while she apologized over and over for how dinner ended.

The Scotts have had a lot of crappy holidays. But this one was, by far, the worst.

Presently, I find myself sitting amid even more chaos than last Thanksgiving. But instead of yelling and tears, everyone is laughing and joking and smiling.

A real family. Noel has a *real* family—with sisters and a brother who all seem to like each other. Even their in-laws seem to fit in well. His parents appear to still be madly in love after many years together, laughing at each other's jokes and passing looks of admiration between them. There are also six grandkids who are bubbly and giggly and making jokes that Veronica keeps saying are inappropriate for the dinner table, but she does it with a smile, almost like she doesn't care but feels like she should say something because it's her job.

I'd always thought my family was the norm—that's what you see on TV and movies, after all: the crazy, dysfunctional families with all the fighting and bickering. But now, seeing Noel's family, and the similarities to Cami's, I know the truth: my family just sucks.

Everyone here is eating the delicious food that Veronica made—chicken, a cheesy potato dish, salad, and rolls. Not one complaint. No one saying they're on a diet, not one person making insulting remarks. Everyone is just . . . happy.

The house is beautiful. It was built about twelve years ago when Noel was a senior in high school. It's a storybook craftsman-style design. A gabled porch, wood shutters, and a stone-and-shingle exterior. The inside is an open-style plan with vaulted ceilings. There's a lot of warmth here, unlike the cold, modern look of my parents' house.

"Are you okay?" Noel leans over and asks, his breath tickling my ear and sending little, tiny prickles down my neck.

"Yeah," I say, adding a nod for emphasis. I'm okay, but I'm also *not* okay. I've just realized that I've been living in crazy town, while other people—not just Cami—have these glorious, wonderful families.

"You look a little shell shocked. We can be a lot to take. I should have warned you."

"No," I say, taking a breath and putting my family hatred aside. "It's great. Your family is . . . great." I turn my head to look at him.

"Great? More like crazy," he says. I can tell that even though he's attempting to downplay it, he clearly loves his family. "I'm guessing your family dinners aren't like this?"

I shake my head and look at him like he must be mad. "Um, when we do have dinner together, it's either cold and sterile or a complete disaster." Thanksgiving was really the only true disaster meal I can remember with my family, but I'm sure there were others. Typically when we eat together, our dinners are pretty stuffy and boring. Nothing like this.

No, this reminds me so much of Cami's family, with her five brothers and their spouses and her seventeen nieces and nephews. Anytime I have dinner with her, I'm always overwhelmed, but in a good way. Envious of what they have.

I feel the same here as I watch one of Noel's nephews who can't be older than four yell, "Poop!" as loud as he can, the other children's giggles filling the dining room, and Veronica telling him that's not appropriate.

"We have a special guest," she says to the boy, pointing over toward me with her fork. "Let's not scare her away."

"Poop!" he says again, and the chorus of children's laughter fills the room once more.

"Okay, okay," Mayor Holiday, a.k.a. Christopher, says in a commanding voice, a big grin on his face. There's still a bandage above his eyebrow from the fight, and a small bruise under his left eye, but otherwise he looks like his normal bow tie–wearing self. Today's version is red with white polka dots. "Tell us about yourself, Mara," he says once the room has calmed down somewhat.

All worries I had about being recognized by Noel's dad vanished as soon as I was introduced to him. It was clear that he had no recollection of meeting me in the street earlier this week.

"You have pretty hair," a girl, probably around seven, says before I can answer the question.

"Thank you," I say to her.

"I'm visiting from Carson City," I say to Christopher and then quickly add, "in Nevada." I wonder briefly if that will ring a bell from our previous conversation, but nope. It looks like this is new information to him.

"I've been to Aspen Lake," says Noel's younger sister Grace, a forkful of salad hovering close to her face. She's got the same eyes and same light-brown hair as Noel, and I'm pretty sure the boy who keeps yelling out potty words is hers. "It's beautiful."

"It is," I agree.

"What do you do there?" asks Noel's sister named Merry. She looks like a mix of Ivy and Noel.

"I work for my dad," I say, trying to keep it simple.

"What does your dad do?" asks Grace.

I look at Noel and then back at the table. "Marketing," I offer. There. That's not a lie. Just not the whole truth.

"How are you liking Carole Cove?" Christopher asks, satisfied with that answer.

"It's great," I say. I'm not lying. Somehow this town has become more to me than the Christmas-in-my-face nightmare it initially presented. I'm not sure when it all shifted. But, if I'm being totally honest with myself, the man sitting next to me, his hand on the back of my chair, might have something to do with it. However it came to be, I can see why everyone here guards this town with such fervor and why they don't want it to change.

"You're in marketing," Christopher says, with a lift of his chin in my direction. "Since you've had a chance to spend time in our town, what do you think we could do to get more tourists here?"

"Oh," I say, surprised by his question. "I . . . I'm not sure."

"Dad," Ivy chastises. She's sitting next to Pete, who's got Kaden next to him. They look like a happy little family. Especially the way Pete has his arm draped around the back of Ivy's chair. "That's a weird thing to ask someone you barely know."

"I'm just interested," he says. "She's been staying in our town"—he holds his hand out toward me—"so maybe she has some insight?"

"Maybe we need a prince in disguise," Noel says, his voice in my ear making that tingling thing happen again.

I snort out a laugh, but then my eyes go wide, an idea popping into my head. "Actually," I say to Christopher, "I do have a thought." All the adults in the room are looking at me now. "You could advertise your town as a Christmas movie getaway."

The looks have turned from interested to questioning.

I swallow, feeling like maybe I'm stepping on toes here, but I forge ahead. "What I mean is, all of those holiday movies that come out every year? This town captures the same holiday feeling. You could market the town that way. I think people would come far and wide for that. The movies are . . . very popular."

"I've seen a few of those," Grace says, her face contemplative. "I've never put that together, but . . . yeah, I can kind of see it."

Christopher leans back in his chair, rubbing his chin the same way Noel does, running an index finger and thumb slowly down it. He looks up at the corner of the room, his expression thoughtful.

"That's not a bad idea, Dad," Grace tells him. "Maybe you could do some ads portraying the town as a holiday movie getaway."

"Ooh," Merry says. "Or maybe they might come and film some movies here. That might also bring in more tourists."

"That's a great idea," I tell her.

"Hmm, I don't know about all that—the movie stuff," Christopher says, with a flit of his hand toward the table. "I like that you're thinking outside the box, though, Mara."

"Maybe we can save the town that way," Gabriel, Noel's youngest sibling and only brother—who I was told goes by Gabe—pipes in. He hasn't been talking much, as he's been shoveling food in his face since we sat down. He looks like a younger version of Noel.

Christopher shakes his head sadly at Gabe. "Not much we can do about the land sale," he says and then lets out a long exhale. "No, that has to happen. We just have to hope whoever buys it doesn't ruin our town."

I feel Noel's hand brush down the side of my thigh, that prickling sensation now going down my leg at his touch. I look up at him, and he gives me a little knowing smile, and I give him one back.

"Thanks for coming tonight," Noel says as we're nearly back to town.

After we had dessert, which was homemade apple pie—one of my favorites—Noel told me he'd take me back to the inn.

"Thanks for talking me into it," I say. "Your family is great."

"They're not too bad."

I huff out a breath. "Trust me, coming from someone whose family is pretty terrible, you've got a good one."

"Yeah," he says as I look over at his profile, his head bobbing, his lips curved upward. "I do have a good family."

He pulls up in front of the inn and puts his truck in park.

"Well," he says.

"Well," I echo.

I want to invite him in. It's just past eight. We could watch another movie or play cards with Irene and Hattie. We could go up to my room and I could introduce him to *Cosmetics and Crimes*. We could lie on my bed, our heads close together, watching my laptop screen. I could look over at him the same time he looks at me and then . . . *Stop it, Mara.*

"I guess I better go," I say after a few beats of silence, the only sounds the low hum of country music playing on the radio and the rumble of Noel's truck. "Thanks again for tonight. I had a really good time."

"Your idea was a good one, by the way. About what we could do with the town."

I smile at him. "Maybe it could work? I don't know anything about tourism. It just sort of came to me."

"Well, I'll let my dad think about it for a bit and then talk to him. Maybe you and I could brainstorm some ideas?"

"I'd love to," I say. "Not like I'm getting out of here anytime soon." On the drive home, I received a notification that the airport would still be closed tomorrow due to the storm. And unfortunately, more snow is in the forecast. Maybe I'll be stuck here until June after all. For now, I might have to resign myself to the fact that I'll probably be here until the auction. But I'll find a way out after that. The Virgin Islands await.

"Hey," Noel says and takes a breath like he's nervous about something. "Since you're stuck here longer, do you . . . would you want to go on a sleigh ride with me tomorrow?"

"A sleigh ride?" I repeat the words like I've never heard them before. Which is silly, because of course I have. But no one has ever asked me to go on one before. Heathen Steven's idea of fun was to go axe throwing. Which is fun the first time, but after the tenth time, it just feels like throwing an axe.

"Yeah, we have a place that does horse-drawn rides. I worked there back in high school."

"Oh." I nod my head. "That sounds . . . amazing."

"Okay," he says. "Around one, then? Does that work for you?"

I cock my head to the side. "But wait, aren't you going to be busy taking care of the town tomorrow?" My voice is teasing, but I'm also wondering.

"I think the town will manage okay," he says, a little smirk on his face.

"Okay, then," I say, going to reach for the door handle.

Before I open the door, and before I can overthink it, I lean over the large cab of the truck toward Noel and plant a kiss on his cheek, letting my lips linger there for longer than the quick mistletoe kisses we've given each other.

"Wow, and no mistletoe, even," Noel says as I pull away. His hand goes up to the spot where my lips just were.

"Nope, that one was because I wanted to." I give him a big smile as I move to open the door.

I hop out of the truck before I do something even crazier like lean over and grab him by his jacket and . . . nope, not going there. I need to stop these thoughts running through my head. Noel and I can't be anything more than friends. That's all we can ever be.

"You didn't kiss him?" Cami says over the phone as I lay back on my bed. I called her as soon as I got back to my room. She filled me in on everything happening back at home, and I told her about my evening with Noel's family.

"No," I say, my voice a protest. "I'm not kissing Noel." No matter how much I want to.

"But you're ruining the movie again," she whines.

I let out a breath. "I live in Carson City, and he lives here."

She sighs. "I guess so. But what about happily ever after? Love against all odds?"

I laugh at her cheesy lines. "I'm thinking that the odds are stacked too high against us in this movie. You're not going to get the happily ever after you were hoping for. Sorry, Cam."

"Oh fine," she says.

"At least one of us is getting a happily ever after," I say, referring to her and Noah.

"Don't get ahead of yourself," she says. "This is a happily ever beginning. I don't know about 'after' yet. Now"—she stops to take a breath—"the question is, will you get out of this town in time for the Virgin Islands?"

"That's a hella yes," I say. "They'll dig out the airport in Missoula soon enough. Or if I have to ride out of here on a horse, I'll do it."

She giggles. "Maybe Santa can give you a lift."

"That's also an option. However it happens, soon enough we'll be lying on the beach."

"Can't wait."

Chapter Twelve

The next day, dressed in my warmest clothes, I'm waiting at the coffee shop for Noel. He asked me to meet him because he was running late and needed to grab something from the shop before we left.

Ivy is making me one of those peppermint-and-white-chocolate lattes while I wait.

"What are you and Noel doing?" she asks after I tell her I'm meeting him here.

"Um . . . he's taking me on a sleigh ride," I tell her, feeling weird saying it out loud and to his sister, of all people.

Her eyebrows move up her forehead. "Really?"

"Yeah, he said he used to work at the place when he was in high school."

She tilts head to the side as if she'd forgotten about that. "Huh," she says, her tone indicating she has some thoughts on the subject.

"Should I be worried? Does Noel know what he's doing?"

"Oh yeah, he knows what he's doing. I just can't believe he's doing it."

I scrunch my forehead. "How's that?"

She twists her mouth to the side, as though she's not sure she should say anything. "I told you—he rarely does anything for himself. Case in point, he's been building a house for two years that's basically just a frame."

I don't have a response to that. I give her a thin smile.

"Well," she says, grabbing a towel and wiping down the espresso machine. "It's a good thing you came to this town, Mara."

This makes my heart sink a little. Noel and I are on the same page, I'm sure. He knows I'm leaving; he knows this can't go anywhere. I don't want his family getting hopeful over something that can never happen.

"Now if we could just find someone for Pete," she says.

"Oh, Noel and I . . ."

"I don't know what I'm going to do about him," she continues talking about Pete as if she didn't even hear my protest. She stares at something in the distance, her eyes going out of focus.

Curiosity getting the better of me, I ask, "What's Pete's story?"

"Pete," she says, bringing her focus back to the espresso machine. "He moved back here from Seattle, around the same time as Noel—just after Kyle died. They were best friends, you know. The three of them."

I nod my head. I knew this because Noel had told me while we were out plowing roads.

"I was glad they were here at first—they were a huge support. But then I expected them to go back to their lives: back to Billings for Noel, and Seattle for Pete. Instead, they've moved back here, to nowheresville. Noel, doing all the things Kyle used to do for the town, and Pete . . . well, Pete has just been a good friend."

"He seems great with Kaden," I say.

"He's the best," she says, concentrating on the machine in front of her. "Kaden loves him."

The bells on the door swing open, and as if our conversation conjured them, Kaden and Pete walk in, hand in hand.

When he sees Ivy, Kaden lets go of Pete's hand and runs over to her, and she lifts him up into a hug.

"Good to see you again, Mara," Pete says as he approaches, giving me a little wave and then pushing his square-rimmed glasses up his nose. He's a cute guy with his full head of dark-brown hair and a nice, angled jaw. He's kind of on the lanky side, but it only seems to add to his charm.

"You too," I say. I didn't get to talk to Pete all that much at dinner last night like I'd wanted. I would have liked to fish around a little about him and Ivy. Probably for the best that I didn't. It's not really my place.

"What did you and Uncle Pete do?" Ivy asks Kaden.

"He took me to Frosty's." I remember seeing that store a few doors down from here. It's a cute little gift store. "Look!" Kaden says as he pulls a little white fidget spinner out of his pocket. "Pete got it for me."

"Pete," Ivy chastises. "You spoil him."

Pete holds up his hands, feigning innocence. "It was cheap."

She gives him one of those what-am-I-going-to-do-with-you looks.

I just stand here and watch the three of them. Looking like the perfect little family. Someone has to have said something to them. I can't be the only one who sees this.

The door rings again, and my heart does a little pitter-patter thing when I see it's Noel. He's in winter boots and jeans, and he's wearing the same navy-blue puffer jacket he's had on the past few times I've seen him.

"Hey," he says, approaching us. "You ready to go, Mara?"

"Yes," I say.

"I've got snow pants in the truck for you."

"Thanks," I say, grateful for his thoughtfulness.

He turns to Ivy. "Did you get the stuff I asked for?"

She gives him a mischievous grin, her lips curling up on only one side "Why, yes I did," she coos, her voice a tease. "I didn't realize what it was for." She gives me a very poignant look.

"Just hand it over," he says, annoyed.

She gives him one of those cooling-and-heating bags, which looks to be pretty heavy.

"Thanks," he says to her and then turns to me. "Ready?"

"Sure," I say.

With a wave to Ivy, Kaden, and Pete, I follow Noel out of the shop.

"What's in the bag?" I ask as the door shuts behind us.

"You'll find out," he says, giving me a little wink.

An hour later, I'm sitting next to Noel on a red two-person sleigh behind a big, beautiful black horse named Fancy. A sheepskin blanket covers our laps as Noel holds the reins, guiding the horse effortlessly through the snow.

It's incredibly gorgeous outside; the sky is blue with delicate, feathery clouds that look as if someone took a paintbrush to them. The ground is a pristine white from the snow, sparkling like diamonds as it reflects the bright afternoon sun.

I've been taking pictures with my phone. Of the sleigh and the horse, of Noel and me, of the surroundings. This is one of those experiences that you never want to forget, that you kind of want to last forever.

The bag Ivy gave Noel, as it turns out, had two large thermoses of hot chocolate, and a couple of muffins from the shop.

Noel slows Fancy down as he pulls back on her reins, and we stop in the middle of a meadow. Beautiful untouched snow covers the ground, and the contrast of the evergreen trees that wrap around the exterior make it all seem a little too good to be true, like something out of a fairy tale. There's barely a sound to be heard, except for a couple of winter birds chirping and some snorting from Fancy, our traveling companion.

"Wow," I say as I take it all in.

"Pretty, right? I've been here plenty of times, and it never gets old. In the summer, this meadow is filled with wildflowers."

"Do they do carriage rides in the summer?"

He shakes his head. "No, tourism slows down here in the summer."

"Seems like a waste," I say, imagining a summer day here with the field full of flowers, the bright-blue sky above, and the fresh, clean air.

"That's what David Bersham wants to do with the town," Noel says, looking out toward the trees. "He thinks we need to develop the town into a summer getaway capitalizing on the lake."

I pull my brows inward. "That doesn't sound like a bad idea."

Noel sniffs, his red nose crinkling as he does. "It would take a lot of money, a lot of investing from the city to do it, according to my dad. And there's no proof that it would work. I think if the idea came from anyone else, maybe my dad might consider it."

"But because it's from David, he thinks it's a bad idea," I say.

"Any idea David has is a bad one to my dad," says Noel.

"Old men and their pride," I say, thinking of my own dad.

Noel lets out a breath, and it swirls around in the cold air.

"Are you . . . ," I start, but then stop myself.

"What?" he asks, looking over at me.

I twist my lips to the side, wondering if I should say anything. "Are you happy you moved back to the town?"

He knits his brows together. "Yes . . . yeah, of course," he says.

"Ivy thinks you moved back for her," I say.

"She told you that?" He shakes his head, sounding irritated, and then looks at the sky and then back down to me. "I mean, that's why I came back at first. Kyle's death was . . . well, it's still pretty devastating. But after being back, I realized this is where I belong. My life was too busy in Billings. I never had time for myself."

"And you do here?" I ask him, my conversation with Ivy running through my mind. Also, I've seen how busy he is with my own eyes.

"Yeah," he says, dipping his chin just once.

"You seem pretty busy to me," I say.

He huffs out a chuckle. "I don't mind this kind of busy. It feels like it's on my own terms here. The city felt stifling. It wasn't for me. I'm definitely cut out for small-town life."

I smile, wagging my head. "But what about Target?"

"You and Target," he says, doing that slow, rumbling chuckle that does funny things to my insides. "Some of us don't need it."

I fake a shudder. "Only bumpkins. Us regular people need Target."

"Did you just call me a bumpkin?"

I push out my lips, giving him my best overconfident look. "I did," I say.

"You think I'm unsophisticated?" He puts his hand on the back of the sleigh right behind me and leans in toward me, a determined look on his face.

"I do," I say, keeping up the pretense, even though my heart has started pumping wildly in my chest as I feel his breath on my lips. He moves in closer, his eyes darting down to my mouth.

He's going to kiss me. I know it. He's going to kiss me and I'm going to let him. Out here in this meadow under the winter sky, in a horse-drawn sleigh. Possibly the most romantic moment of my life.

Just as he's about to erase the distance between us, Fancy lets out a loud snort and we both look at her just in time to see her tail rise. Then she does something very unromantic right in front of us.

"Lovely," Noel says, the spell between us broken. He reaches up and pats Fancy on the rear, which causes her to teeter and move forward a couple of steps, yanking the sleigh with her. He shakes his head at the horse, snarling a half smile at her.

I feel like if this were a movie, Noel would recognize the moment by saying something like, "Good timing, Fancy." But he doesn't; he lifts up the reins and directs her to take off again, pulling us through the meadow.

This isn't a movie, and Fancy's little display was an awakening, albeit a gross one. But it snapped us back into reality. I can't kiss Noel. I can't give in to these feelings I know are growing for him. He knows it too. If he thought it would work, he would have kissed me the other night at the inn. But he's too good of a guy to risk it.

No, I know nothing can happen here, and I'm okay with it. Soon this whole town, Noel, and all the feelings I've had will be a part of my past.

Chapter Thirteen

"The governor has declared most of Montana in a state of emergency as the winter storm continues. Upwards of forty-eight inches have fallen on the city of Missoula, and businesses will continue to stay closed as plows attempt to dig out the town."

I turn off the news station, muttering words under my breath that I'm sure Hattie and Irene would find offensive. I'm in the movie room of the inn, back in my heart thermals and the black hoodie Cami gave me. I didn't bother putting on any makeup today. I'm just going to wallow here, perhaps until I'm old and gray, since I'll probably never get out of this town.

In reality, it looks like I'm going to have to just wait it out until the auction. There's no reason for me to fly home, even if they open the airport in the next couple of days. The auction is only four days away. It's fine; I can stay here longer. If only I weren't feeling so freaking bored right now. And if I'm being honest with myself, a little blue.

I send texts to my parents and to Cami informing them that I won't be coming back any time soon. I get no reply from my dad, which is to be expected (he's not a texter) and an "oh honey!" from my mom. Cami sends me three words: "Good. Kiss him."

I send her back the red-face cussing emoji. I can't kiss Noel—I explained all the reasons why to her last night after returning from the sleigh ride. After he and I had basically had a DTR—define the relationship—as we drove back to town.

"I had a great time today," I'd said once we settled in the cab of his truck driving down the two-lane road leading back to Main Street.

"I'm glad," he said, looking at me for a second before his eyes went back to the road. "I did too."

"I'm . . . happy I met you, Noel," I said. I wanted to say so much more, but it's all that came out of my mouth.

"I feel the same. I'm glad you got stuck here."

I laughed. I couldn't imagine getting stuck in any other town that would have me smiling like this one did.

"I wish . . . ," he started.

"Yes?" I wanted him to say something, but *what*, I wasn't really sure. *I wish . . . we didn't live so far apart. I wish . . . we had met under different circumstances. I wish . . . they would just invent teleportation already.* I mean, honestly, what's the freaking holdup, science?

He let out a breath. "I don't know what I wish. Maybe that we had more time."

I looked down at my gloved hands resting in my lap and smiled. "I wish that too."

"I really like spending time with you, Mara," he said, risking a glance at me before looking back at the road.

"I like spending time with you," I say.

"If things were different . . ."

"I know," I say, stopping him.

After a few beats of silence, he asked, "If flights open up tomorrow, will you leave?"

I knew what he was asking here—If I had the choice, would I stay? The truth is, I didn't know. I'd been going back and forth between wishing the airport would be open the next day and wishing I could be stuck here longer.

"I don't know," I said, feeling an empty sensation swirl around in a stomach full of hot chocolate and muffins.

He let out a breath. "Well, it's just as well. I'm going to be pretty busy the next couple of days," he said. "I won't have a ton of time."

"I get it," I said. This was starting to feel like a breakup. Which was ridiculous.

"I feel like it's probably for the best, since . . . everything," he said.

"I understand." I knew what "everything" meant. I'd leave this town eventually, whether it was the next day or after the auction. The more time we spent together, the harder it was going to be. Sure, we could text and talk on the phone when I got back to Carson City. We could have some sort of friendship. But then what?

He parked his truck in front of the inn and walked me to the door of my current residence. I almost didn't want him to; I knew what was coming, and I wanted to put it off. But as we stood by the entrance, before I could even touch the handle, Noel grabbed me and pulled me into a hug.

There are hugs with gentle arms that feel kind of like the knockoff brand—like you're only getting half of what someone is capable of. And then there are the ones that are nearly bone crushing, that tell you everything you need to know without words. It was one of those hugs. Essentially, it was a goodbye hug.

So, the relationship was defined: we didn't have one. And Noel was finding it too hard to keep doing what we were doing. I am too, to be honest. Not enough to stop spending time with him, but Noel clearly knows what's best for him. He's a good guy. A bad one would have kissed me despite the consequences, to take what he wanted. And anyway, good guys are probably really bad kissers. Now I'm just deluding myself.

Oh well. It's official: I'm stuck here, in Carole Cove. Again. At least I now know the real reason I was starting to fall for this town. It was all Noel. Because now that we've said goodbye for like the third time, this place seems dreary, and all the Christmas decor is making me itchy and full of hate again.

Case in point, the Garland Mercantile sells yarn, and after breakfast I walked over there and bought a ridiculous number of skeins. Everyone is getting a hate scarf this year. Including Cami. I blame her for all these thoughts in my head. She's the one who built up this whole movie thing, who keeps telling me I need to just kiss Noel already.

I know it's not her. It's Noel himself that's the problem. Or maybe it's the attraction I feel to him. Like my heart is literally pulling toward him, like we're magnets, drawn to each other.

Maybe I'll make myself my own rage scarf. It will be in that hideous shade of greenish brown. Or what some people in my Facebook crochet group call "lung tar." That's a perfect color for how I'm feeling. Drab brown, with a hint of green.

"Knock, knock," says Hattie from the doorway, rapping on the frame twice.

"Hello," I say, disappointed it wasn't Noel. My heart was recovering from the little jumping thing it had done in my chest. Hoping . . . wishing. And now I'm just annoyed with myself for even thinking it.

"Fancy a game of gin rummy?" she asks.

It's like Irene and Hattie know what's going on with me and Noel, the thing that really can't be defined. It wasn't a breakup, or a friend zone thing. It was just . . . nothing. No relationship whatsoever. That's what we decided on.

They must sense something because they've both been extra sweet today. Making me a yummy omelet for breakfast with some fresh buttermilk biscuits and that amazing raspberry-peach jam, which I ate until I was sick.

Because I have nothing else to do, I agree to play cards. I get up from my lazy slouch on the red-and-green plaid couch in the movie room and follow her to the front room, where Irene is already setting up the table.

This is my life now. At least for the next four days. Eating until I'm sick and playing cards with two cute old ladies. Oh, and rage crocheting. Can't forget that.

We play three rounds of gin rummy, with the sisters giving me all the town gossip, none of which I care about except for one little tidbit. David Bersham is pulling his bid for the land.

I should be thrilled about this since, according to Michael, he was our biggest competition. I guess I am, but I'm also curious as to why he'd pull out. Was it an act of goodwill because of the fight? A waving of a white flag? He was so adamant about the land at the auction, it doesn't seem like he'd just pull out like that.

Regardless, after winning the third round of gin rummy, I go up to my room and shoot off a text to Michael telling him this potentially good news.

He sends me back one word: "Good."

He hasn't said much to me since I turned him down after the auction. I feel quite proud of myself for doing that. It's growth.

In need of some fresh air, I throw on some black leggings, my cream coat, my Heathen Steven scarf, and my Hunter boots and take a stroll down Main Street with a crime podcast in my ears as I peruse. It's a cold, overcast day with the storm still raging south of here. Carole Cove and the surrounding towns haven't gotten much since the initial storm. But every once in a while, I see a single snowflake drift slowly down from the sky.

Feeling daring, or maybe having a death wish, I risk a visit to the Uncheerful Baker and buy a chocolate croissant. I also get some scornful looks, free of charge. She must have recognized me from the last time I was here because she didn't attack me with assumptions like she did before. Still, the woman scares me. I hurry out of there as fast as I can.

I continue walking down the street, and I'm just about to walk past the Merry Little Coffee Shop, but I stop myself before anyone can see me through the window of the store. I could go in there. I could go inside and pretend like everything is all good. Get myself a caramel-and-hazelnut latte, which sounds amazing right now. Chances are, Noel isn't even there. And if he is, so what? We're . . . nothing. And if we're nothing, then I should be able to get a latte, right?

I'm about to take the final steps toward the entrance and go inside when the door swings open and out comes Noel, his breath making clouds in the cold air. I should spin around and walk back to the inn and hope he didn't see me, but instead, I'm frozen in my spot. Like my feet are cemented.

Apparently Noel is experiencing the same thing, frozen to his spot, because he's just standing there looking at me.

"Hey," I finally say, giving him a little wave and a small smile. I reach up and take my earbuds out and put them in my pocket.

"Hey there," he says, returning the smile — it's small, and not a dimple in sight.

He's got his hands in the pockets of that black wool coat he wore over his suit after the auction. This time, it's over jeans and a black sweater.

"What're you listening to?" he asks.

"A crime podcast," I say.

His lips pull up into a smile. "I thought so."

"I was thinking," he says at the same time I say, "What have you . . ."

We stop and do that awkward thing we've done before, and it feels like déjà vu, each of us offering for the other to go first.

"You were thinking?" I finally ask.

Noel takes a few steps toward me so now we're standing about a foot apart.

He tilts his head a little to the side. "I was actually on my way to the inn."

"You were?"

"Yeah. I just had this thought. Kind of like an epiphany." I watch as a snowflake flutters down, landing on his jacket, and then disappears, melting into the wool.

"An epiphany?" I ask.

"Yeah." He gives me a smile without teeth. "We could be friends, right? I mean, we're both adults. And you're staying until the auction now, aren't you?"

I nod. He must have heard the airport is still closed. Or maybe he purposefully looked it up. Either way, it makes butterflies take flight in my stomach. He's been thinking about me today. Maybe even as much as I've been thinking of him.

"Yep," I say. "I'm staying until the auction."

"Okay, well, this town can be pretty dull," he says, his nose and cheeks starting to turn red in the cold.

I huff out a laugh. "Um, you just called this town dull." I pretend to look around me like someone might have heard him. The sidewalk is mostly empty around us.

The corners of his lips pull upward. "I meant for you, because you don't live here. And you're stuck at a bed-and-breakfast." He reaches up and scratches the back of his neck, his cheeks turning that cute shade of pink again. "What I mean is, we should at least hang out while you're here. As friends. What do you think?"

"Didn't you say you were busy?"

He looks down at the ground and then back at me. "I do have some things to do, but . . . they can wait."

My lips want to move upward, but I keep them down, setting my face as seriously as I can. "I don't know," I say.

Noel looks taken aback. "You . . . don't know."

I look to the side like I'm contemplating. "I don't think I could be friends with a bumpkin." I give him a little lift of my shoulders and push my lips outward.

He smiles, a big one, both dimples making an appearance this time. I drop the facade and give him one of my best in return.

"I'll work on trying not to be such a bumpkin," he says. "No guarantees."

"So, what was your plan, then? After figuring out this friend thing." I point to him and then me. The "friend" word feels a little acrid on my tongue, to be honest. But if this is all I can have with Noel, then I'll take it. Cami will be disappointed; she'll tell me no one would want to watch this movie. But boring ending aside, I'm up for spending as much time as I can with Noel, even as his friend, seeing that I spent the first half of today thinking I wouldn't get to see him at all, and it was just short of torturous.

"I thought you might want to see my house," he says. "Or at least the foundation of my house."

"Okay," I say. "I'd like to see your house."

He lets out a breath. "Want to go now?"

"This is it," Noel says as we park in front of a large lot. There's a small old-fashioned, blue-trimmed craftsman bungalow home to the left, and the cement foundation and most of the framing for the first level of what looks to be a fairly large house, front and center.

The lot backs up to a foothill covered with trees and brush. I can see why he picked this spot — it's pretty stunning. The agent in me wants to know what he paid for it, but I hold myself back. I do know that a lot this size in Aspen Lake would go for a pretty penny.

We get out of the truck and Noel walks me over to the foundation, which looks to have been recently shoveled, along with a little path through the snow to get there. "The entrance." He ushers me inside what will someday be a doorway.

"Why thank you," I play along.

He takes me on a tour, telling me where everything will be. An entryway with an office to the right, a closet on the left. Through a hallway that leads into a great room with a kitchen, and a living room area. I pepper him with real estate-y questions about the lot and the build to satisfy my inner agent.

"I think it'll be amazing," I say as we stand close together in the middle of where Noel's just told me his contemporary-style kitchen will be.

"Someday, when I finish it, of course," he says.

"You plan to do it all yourself?"

He looks down at the cement floor, scuffing it with his boot.

"No; I'd wanted to do quite a bit of it, but it's taken a lot of time to get this much done. I'm bringing in someone after Christmas."

"It's taken you two years to get to this point?" I ask, looking around at only cement and framing. I knew this because Ivy had filled me in. But it seemed like she might have been exaggerating, trying to drive her point home that Noel does nothing for himself. Apparently, she hadn't been.

He reaches up and rubs the back of his neck. "Yep," he says.

"What's taken so long? Is it all your princely duties?"

He gives me a little smile and a one-shoulder shrug. "Well, yeah. But really, it's just . . . life. I've hardly had time to work on it."

I cock my head to the side, studying him. "Didn't you say one of the reasons you left Billings was because it was a lot?" I believe his exact word was *stifling*.

"Yeah?"

"Well, it seems to me you're just as busy here. I thought the point of moving back to the small town after leaving the big city was to slow down and experience life. That's how it works in those holiday movies, at least." I give him a closed-mouth smile.

He chuckles. "Yeah, I guess you're right."

"I think Ivy might be right. You need to take more time for yourself," I say.

"Maybe."

"Not maybe," I say. "As your *friend*" —I exaggerate the word a little—"I think you should listen to her. She said . . ." I stop myself, not sure if I should say what I want to say.

"She said what?"

I fold my arms in front of me, unsure if I should say this out loud but now feel like I have to. "She thinks you're trying to pick up where Kyle left off."

He shakes his head. "Did she say that? That's not what I'm doing." He doesn't sound mad, like I had half expected him to be. Like people usually are when you call them out on their stuff. I wonder if someone like Noel could ever get mad.

"Are you sure about that?" I ask.

"I like to be busy," he says, giving me a shrug. "And sure, Kyle left a hole in this town when he died. So if I get to help out, then that's a win-win for me."

He puts his hands in his pockets and kicks the ground again with his boot.

I nod, wondering if Ivy's worry for her brother might be in vain. His reasoning seems logical to me.

"My moving back here after Kyle died doesn't have to have all this meaning. I'm not trying to bring him back or replace him around the town like Ivy thinks. I just wanted to be here. I miss him, of course. But I'm happier here. I belong here."

"I believe you," I say. "You're the prince of Carole Cove, after all."

He snorts out a laugh and looks around his future house. "Besides," he begins, "builders start next month on this place." He gestures around us with his hands. "So now that's taken care of. If I stopped helping around the town, what would I fill my time with then?"

"I don't know," I say. "You could knit."

He does that chuckling thing—the one I can feel in my bones. "Sounds like a good use of time."

"Oh, it is. I could teach you the art of rage crocheting," I say.

He furrows his brow. "Rage crocheting?"

"Yes," I say, bobbing my head up and down. "It's very therapeutic."

"I'm sure," he says, the chuckle turning into a laugh as he shakes his head like he's not sure what to do with me. I wonder if Noel has ever been mad enough at someone to feel that kind of rage, to have the *need* to take his feelings out on something.

"Or," I say, "you could write that great American novel you've always wanted to write."

"Definitely not on my bucket list."

"Invent something?"

He shakes his head.

"Well, what do you want to do, then? What does Noel Holiday want?"

Noel's smile falls then, his eyes studying my face. He takes a step forward and then stops himself, like he's questioning what he's thinking right now. But then he leans in and snakes an arm around my waist, pulling me into him with his hand on my back.

"Wh . . . what are you doing?" I ask, our faces close together, my heart racing. His other hand comes up and rests on my cheek, his fingers gently caressing my cold skin, like I'm something precious, something to treasure.

"Noel?" I question, wanting him to close the gap between us so badly and also scared that, like before, he won't do it.

"I'm showing you what I want," he says, his eyes moving to my mouth.

"What you want?" I ask, my voice breathy as my heart pounds in my chest.

"Yes," he says.

Then his lips are on my lips. Tender at first, then more exploratory as his mouth moves over mine. I kiss him back, and it only takes a few seconds for the blood to rush to our lips, warming them up.

My entire body is heating up, in fact, especially as the hand that was on my cheek moves to my neck and his fingers weave into my hair. He leans me back slightly, deepening the kiss. I wrap my arms around his waist, pulling myself into him so there's not a millimeter of space between us. His tongue sweeps my bottom lip and then dips into my mouth, and I feel like I'm falling, grateful to have his steadying arm around me, holding me to him.

I've never been thoroughly kissed like this, never in my life. Never with so much tenderness and feeling. All the other kisses I've had before felt like something was being taken from me, not given to me.

This is not how I imagined a good guy would kiss. I thought it would be more timid and careful. Not intense and life altering like this is. I think I'd like this moment to last forever. We can stay in the middle of this unfinished house, kissing until we turn old and gray.

Like a movie, a montage of my time with Noel goes through my mind while he continues to move his mouth over mine, both arms now wrapped around me. I see everything that got us to this point. The mistletoe he kissed me under, seeing him at the coffee shop, my car stuck in the mud, catching me at the auction, playing bridge with the sisters, sitting in the cab of his truck while plowing roads, watching a cheesy holiday movie, a sleigh ride through a quiet meadow. And then . . . here.

If this were a movie, then this would be the money shot—the culmination of all our feelings, of everything that got us here, standing on a slab of concrete with Noel's arms around me, his mouth covering mine, our souls connecting.

I can't even think about what comes next, because I don't even care.

Chapter Fourteen

"THIS IS THE BEST NEWS EVER!" Cami yells into the phone. I'm lying in my bed in my pajamas that I just put back on, even though it's late afternoon. This is the first time I've gotten to talk to Cami all day because she's been busy with Noah and I didn't want to tell her over text about my kiss with Noel yesterday. Now she's being way over-the-top about it. At one point, she even busted out singing the "Hallelujah Chorus," and I had to pull the phone away from my ear so I didn't end up with hearing loss.

"Are you happy with my movie now?" I ask.

"I'm *so* happy," she squeals. "I've been rooting for you two this whole time."

"I know," I say, smiling into the phone. Then my smile drops as I ask her my next question. The one that's been weighing on my mind. "But, Cam, what happens next? This is all so complicated."

After the kiss to end all kisses, Noel and I went to his little bungalow house and he made me some dinner. Then we talked and snuggled and kissed like teenagers on his brown leather couch until I made him take me back to the inn, before it became too awkward for me to sneak back in. Irene and Hattie would have had a field day with that.

We never talked about what happens next. I don't think either of us wanted to bring it up. I know I didn't, and I slept horribly last night because I couldn't turn my brain off.

Just because we've given into our feelings and kissed, doesn't change anything about all the reasons it was a bad idea in the first place. I still live in Carson City, and he still lives here in Carole Cove. After Saturday, after the auction, I'll be leaving here and going to the Virgin Islands with Cami. And then . . . what?

"Don't overthink it," Cami says. "Just let things happen and see where it all goes."

I let out a breath. It feels like I haven't taken a good deep one since Noel's lips touched mine for the first time. My mind and body feel all haywire. I think I need a nap.

"Okay," I say. "Yes, that's good advice. I shouldn't get ahead of myself." A kiss doesn't mean happily ever after in real life like it does in Hallmark movies. It means . . . well, I don't know yet. Right now, it just means that Noel and I kissed. That's it. But oh, what a kiss it was.

"So is he a good kisser?" Cami asks.

"Best ever," I say.

"Really?" She's doing that squealing voice again.

"Yes, really. Like, he puts Heathen Steven to shame." I roll to my back so I'm looking up at the popcorn ceiling.

She makes a sound like a cat coughing up a hair ball. "Gross," she says. "I told you that you could do better than him."

"You did," I say. "And you were right."

"And I was right about Noel," she says.

"I wouldn't go that far. We still have no idea where this is going."

"Stop! Stop thinking about it."

Right. She's right. I wish she were here, in person, to keep reminding me. Maybe I can keep her on the phone all day so every time my mind goes there, she can tell me to stop. My own personal guidance counselor.

My phone chimes, indicating I have a new text. I pull the phone away from my ear and look at my screen to see that it's from Noel. We exchanged numbers last night and it felt strange that we hadn't done so already.

"Hold on," I say to Cami. "That's him texting."

I hear her squealing again as I pull up my texting app and read what he's sent.

Noel: Still here. Hopefully leaving in an hour.

I look at the top of my phone screen and see that it's nearly four.

Me: Okay, drive safe

Noel: Can I see you when I get home?

I send him the little thinking emoji.

Me: Let me think about it . . . yes

Noel: Good answer

I stare at my phone, smiling at it like a starstruck teenager. Noel had something he couldn't get out of today, and the roads were clear enough for him to drive to the next town over, to the county building with his dad to file some paperwork.

166

He asked me to go with, but I thought it would be weird with his dad there, so I opted to stay here. Although now I'm wishing I would have just gone, awkward or not. Between the stuff he had to do at the coffee shop this morning and then this visit to the county building, that's a lot of time to spend apart when we have so little time left.

Plus, I can only fill my day with so many games of gin rummy and so much crocheting. I did do a little bit of work today, but my head has been in the clouds, so not much has gotten done. Also, my crocheting really suffers when it's void of rage. I'm all slow and happy about it, and it takes forever. At least Noel is on his way back now and I'll get to see him soon.

I hold my phone to my chest and sigh.

"Hello? Mara?" I hear a tinny sounding voice say.

"Crap!" I say, putting the phone to my ear. "Cami?"

"You forgot about me," she says, her tone flat.

"No, I didn't," I lie. I totally did. My brain really is in a different place.

"I forgive you. What did he say?"

I sigh. "He wants to see me when he gets back."

"Yes!" She says, and I tell her I need to go before she starts up with the "Hallelujah Chorus" again.

I wake up to a noise at my window. Like someone is throwing something at it. I don't even know what time it is, or when I fell asleep, but I do remember a very vivid crime story I listened to once that started with someone tapping on a window.

Do I hide under the bed? Call the police? I decide to do my own due diligence first and crawl over to the window. I peek out of the bottom corner, and I can't really see anything. It's dark outside, but I should be able to see what's making that noise with the streetlamp and the soft glow of the inn's Christmas lights.

Something hits the window again, and I stifle a scream. But I lift my head up a little more and peer out. There's no deck or anything for anyone to hide on—in fact, it's just a straight shot down from my window. I move my head up just a little more, and then I see something. There's someone down there, standing just a few feet in front of the streetlamp.

I stand up because I know who it is. I open the window, and it creaks and moans and gets stuck a few times before I can open it fully. Because there's no screen, I pop my head out into the frigid night air. "Noel?"

"Hey," he says, in a stage whisper.

"What's going on . . . What are you doing down there?" I say, using the same stage whisper, and then I wonder why we're talking like this. How late is it? Are people asleep?

I remember then that I was supposed to see him after he finished the work he was doing with his dad at the county office, and I must have fallen asleep while waiting.

"I've been trying to get ahold of you," he says, still using the stage whisper.

"I never got a call from you."

"I called and I texted," he says, putting his hands on his hips.

That's strange, I don't remember my phone ringing. I must have been in a deep sleep. It makes sense after all the tossing and turning I did last night.

"Well, what are you doing down there? Just come inside. I'll meet you downstairs."

He smiles at me. "I've got a better idea."

"You do?"

Noel traipses through the snow and stops just below my room. I watch as he starts to climb the trellis that runs from the bottom of the house all the way up to my window.

"Are you crazy?" I yell down to him. "There's probably ice all over that, and you don't know how sturdy it even is."

"Yes, I do," he says, sounding breathy as he makes the climb up the wall. Like he's Spider-Man or something. "I installed it myself last summer."

"Of course you did," I say, rolling my eyes even though he can't see me. "Just hurry up." I'm starting to giggle at how ridiculous this is. Like we're teenagers and he's sneaking into my house after my parents have gone to sleep. Which may have been a fantasy when I was younger.

"Hey there," he says when he reaches my room, just his head peeking over the window ledge. "I like the outfit."

I look down at myself. I'm still in my pajamas from when I changed into them earlier. It's just a pair of pajama shorts and a pink T-shirt. I had planned to change before I saw Noel, but apparently I fell asleep instead.

I shake my head and chuckle at him peeking in through my window, all my teenage fantasies coming true. "You idiot," I say. "Just get in here already. I'm freezing."

He climbs the rest of the way into my room, and then he's just standing there in front of me. I can't believe Noel Holiday climbed up a trellis to my room and through the window. His cheeks and his nose are red from the cold, and he has that very distinct smell of someone who's been outside in the cold of winter.

"I've always wanted to do that," he says.

"You've always wanted to climb up the trellis you put in last summer? Or sneak into a girl's window after curfew?" I say the last line in my best seductive voice, which really sounds more like someone who smokes two packs a day. I should work on that.

Noel looks at me strangely. "Sneak into a window, of course. And it's only nine," he says.

I huff out a breath. "You're ruining my fantasy."

"You had a curfew at nine?" He pulls his brows inward.

"Just shut up and kiss me," I demand.

And so he does. He pulls me into him, wrapping his arms around me, his lips on mine. He feels so cold in contrast to my toasty-warm self, who's been all cozy under the duvet on my bed. Now I remember that I had turned on some *Cosmetics and Crimes* while I was waiting for him and then dozed off.

I should be annoyed that I missed out on more time with him because I fell asleep, but as his kiss deepens, sending rapid-fire tingles down my spine, I can't bring myself to care. He's here now.

He does a little sucking thing on my bottom lip, and there I go turning into Jell-O again. I missed these amazing lips today. His kisses are ruining me for other men. I'll never be able to get over them. How can I go back to my normal life after this? *Stop it, Mara. Don't think of the future.*

The kissing slows, and then he pulls his mouth away from mine, and I instantly feel the loss. I also feel a little dizzy on my feet, my head swimming. Thank goodness he's still got his arms around me.

"Hey," he says, and then he kisses me on the nose.

I smile and then look up at him. "I can't believe you just climbed through my window."

"Romantic, wasn't it? And now Irene and Hattie have no idea I'm here." He waggles his eyebrows at me.

"No gossip then," I say, and he nods. Or hundreds of questions. He's a genius. I bring a finger up to my chin, looking like I'm contemplating. "Whatever shall we do?"

"I can think of a few things," he says, his voice deep and husky.

My breath hitches, and my eyes go wide.

"Relax," he says, a smirk on his face. "I just want to kiss you."

"Right," I say, on a breath.

Right. Of course. This is Noel—he's one of the good guys. He'd never make me feel pressured or rushed to do anything. He's also smart and knows that we can't make this any harder than it's already going to be. And taking this any further will only complicate things more.

I reach up and unzip his coat, keeping my eyes on his as I do. Feeling heat course through my veins as I push it off his shoulders and then let him do the rest. He looks for a place to set it and then just throws it on the floor, like he can't be bothered.

I giggle and then sit on the edge of the bed, maneuvering myself backward, toward my pillow, keeping my eyes on him the entire time. I gesture for him to follow me with my index finger.

He doesn't have to be asked twice. He climbs onto the bed and then crawls toward me until his face is right by mine. Then he lies down, his torso half on me. I wrap an arm around his back and slide it up toward his shoulders, feeling the hard muscles there. His elbow lands on the other side of me, up by my shoulder, and he runs his fingers through my hair. We're face-to-face now, so close. His eyes are intense, like he's the luckiest guy in the world.

"Hi," I say.

"Hi," he says back. Then he dips his head and presses a soft kiss to my lips, then moves to my cheek and down to my chin before stopping at my neck.

I kind of want to freeze time right here, with Noel doing amazing things with his lips on my neck. If only that were a thing, stopping time. We could stay here forever, a never-ending movie. But there's an ending to this one, and it's coming quickly. *Stop it, Mara. Focus on the now.*

Yes, the now. Which is Noel working his way back up my neck leaving soft, light, feathery kisses until he gets to my lips. The hand that was playing with my hair has now moved down my arm and up my side. He digs his fingers lightly into my back as he kisses me thoroughly, our tongues dancing, his mouth making memories with mine.

The now is a very good place to be.

Chapter Fifteen

"I think we should tell my dad why you're in town," Noel says to me the next morning as we sit at the coffee shop.

After kissing for quite a while last night, I made him watch another cheesy movie with me. This one was called *A Very Mistletoe Christmas*. I found it randomly and told him it was meant to be. It was worse than the prince movie, but it was gratifying to snuggle up with Noel on the bed and watch it on my laptop, I don't think either of us minded. I snuck him out the front door after that, not giving into his desire to climb back down the trellis.

This morning I had a quick breakfast with the sisters, who didn't seem to know Noel had been in my room last night, for which I was grateful. I then headed to the coffee shop to meet him. He kissed me, fully on the lips, in front of all the other patrons. There weren't all that many given tourism is at an all-time low due to the storm they're continuing to dig most of the state out of. We definitely got some looks, including one from a very slack-jawed Ivy. And a "Kissing is gross" from Kaden, who was sitting at a table in the corner with Pete.

"You think we should tell your dad that I'm here for the land?" I repeat a version of what he just said. Leaning in just in case anyone could overhear.

He nods. "I have an idea," he says, his eyes looking excited. "I did some research, and I think that if you're able to bring the full amount of the minimum bid to the auction, then they can cancel it and sell the land to your dad."

"Why would your dad do that, though?" I ask, my brows pulled inward. "He stands the chance of getting more for the land if it goes to auction."

"Yes, but he also risks it going to someone who wants to change everything. I think he'd do it, but only if your dad is able to pay the amount in full, no financing."

I look at the paper cup in my hands, running my thumb over the ridges of the sleeve wrapped around it, as I think about what Noel is saying.

"What do you think?" he asks.

I look up from my cup and into his earnest blue eyes. "I know my dad really wants the land. I think he could have the money by then. I'd have to talk to him, though."

Noel's lips pull up into a grand smile, both dimples on full display. "Okay"—he rubs his hands together—"I think we should talk to my dad first and see what he thinks."

I curl my upper lip, my eyes wide. "You want *me* to talk to your dad?" I point a finger at myself. *Is he crazy?*

He bobs his head up and down. "Yeah, I think he'll want to hear it from you."

I'm fully scrunching my brow now, hearing my mom's voice in my head about all the future wrinkles I'll have if I keep it up. "What if he doesn't believe me since I . . ." I pause and lean in toward Noel again; his spicy scent nearly sends me off track, but I pull myself together and whisper, "Since I lied about why I'm here? It might be better coming from just you."

Noel shakes his head. "Trust me, if we can give him an option that will save this town — *his* town — he won't care about any of that."

I twist my lips to the side. "Okay," I say.

"Okay?" he asks, like he didn't think I'd acquiesce so quickly.

"Yes, let's talk to your dad," I say. I feel tendrils of excitement start in my stomach at the thought. This could be the answer to everything. My dad could get the land, I could get the office in Carson City, and Noel and I could . . . *nope. Don't go there, Mara.*

"We got the land," I say to my dad over the phone later that evening, back in my room after leaving Noel so he could get a few things done.

"What?" he asks, his tone indicating he's confused by this news. "I thought the auction was on the twentieth?"

"It is," I say. "I just had a talk with the mayor, and if we can pay the minimum asking price in full on Saturday, then he'll call off the auction."

My dad chuckles into the phone. "Are you serious?"

I smile even though he can't see me. "I'm serious."

"Well done, kiddo," he says. "I'm impressed."

I could tell him that it was actually all Noel. And that, as it turns out, it wasn't all that hard to get his dad on board. In fact, he hardly batted an eye after he found out the real reason I'm in Carole Cove. He just looked at me for a few seconds and then gave me one single nod, and that was it. Then Noel presented him with the plan.

"And your dad doesn't want to do anything with the land?" the mayor had asked, after Noel finished explaining. We were in his office, which was in the back of the town center building where the auction was held, but his space didn't look quite as dilapidated as the room the failed auction had been held in. Still, there was no glamour, considering the plain white walls, an older fake-wood desk, and a well-used office chair where Mayor Holiday sat.

"No," I said, shaking my head, sitting in one of the worn-out chairs that faced his desk, Noel in the other one next to me. "He only has plans to sit on it and let it accrue value."

Mayor Holiday let out a breath. "Then I think this is our best option," he said. "If you can have the money by Saturday, then we'll have a deal."

We all smiled at each other then, the three of us. The mayor let out a jovial laugh, seeming a little giddy at the prospect. He looked to Noel. "This is going to really tick off David Bersham."

Noel just gave him a thin smile, not looking thrilled with his dad's response. When I asked him about it later, Noel said that before the land went to auction, David had offered a cash deal but his dad had turned him down. I found myself wishing I knew the whole story and not just the Holidays' side. Not that it mattered or would even change anything.

I came back to the inn after making the tentative deal with the mayor and called my dad as soon as I closed the door to my room.

"So do you think you can get the money by then?" I ask my dad, who's currently still chuckling into the phone.

"Absolutely," he says. "I'll call Michael right now and get it squared away."

"Good," I say.

"You did it, kiddo. I'm proud of you," he says. "The Carson City office is yours. You deserve it."

"Thanks, Dad," I say. I take in a big breath, waiting for some grand sense of elation to sweep over me. At his feelings of pride, at the office I'll be managing soon. But even after we say goodbye and hang up, I feel more underwhelmed than anything. I don't know why. This is what I've wanted, what I've been working for. Isn't it? Maybe I've had too much excitement already for the day.

Except that can't be true, because I feel a thrill run through me when I look at the time on my phone and see that I have just under two hours before meeting Noel for dinner. We're going to the Chimney Stack, a bar and grill on the other side of Main Street, so I can decide who has the better burger, them or the Jolly Café.

Just a little recap, landing the office in Carson City is not as exciting as I thought it would be, but a burger in a Podunk town in Nowheresville, Montana, brings me joy.

What is happening to me?

Chapter Sixteen

The next morning, I wake up and have breakfast with the sisters. I keep it simple, asking for just one egg and one biscuit because my stomach is still recovering from the greasy thing I ate last night at the Chimney Stack. In the match of who made it best, the Jolly Café wins, hands down.

I'm blaming the food, but I think my stomach is churning for a whole other reason.

After dinner, Noel and I ended up back in my room at the inn, lying on my bed and kissing and talking until we both dozed off in each other's arms. Never once discussing the fact that we're almost to the auction, and what that means. Noel snuck out of the inn sometime before sunrise so he would be gone before the sisters woke up. The bed felt cold after he left, and I lay awake not able to stop my brain from thinking. Or overthinking, really.

The town has been saved; this holiday movie got its happily ever after as far as that's concerned. Cue the campy celebratory music. But what about the hero and the heroine?

No matter which way I slice it, or how I do the math, it all comes down to one answer: nothing. Nothing can happen for Noel and me. I'm leaving the morning after the auction. Then I'm going to the Virgin Islands with Cami for Christmas. When I return, I'm going to be running a busy office in Carson City. Noel will be here, performing his princely duties, building a house that he probably plans to die in.

We'll be living two separate lives, and no matter how I try to make things work in my head, there's no hope for us.

The reality is, we only have two more days, and the auction is tomorrow morning. Even though it's not technically going to be an auction, I still have to show up with Michael and bring proof that we'll be able to fund the purchase right away so they can cancel the bidding. Then we'll sign contracts and that will be the end of it all.

To make matters worse, our grand plan to have my dad buy the land tomorrow now has Noel working with his dad and a real estate attorney on the contract today. Our last full day together, and he won't be available until later this afternoon.

"Noel sure left early this morning," Irene says as she picks up the empty biscuit plate in front of me.

I sigh and lean on my hand at the mention of his name. Then my eyes go wide when I realize what she's just said.

"What?" I say, not sure how to respond. Do I own it? Pretend like I don't know what she's talking about? Why do I suddenly feel like I need a good excuse, a reason why he'd be here? Like I've been caught sneaking my boyfriend out of my room by my parents? Something I never actually did when I was a teenager.

He was fixing my bed. I didn't want to bother you. No, that insinuates so much.

He left his jacket and came by to get it. How could he forget his jacket? In this weather? And at five in the morning?

I look at Irene, she's giving me a knowing smile, and I remember that I'm a grown woman and I paid to rent a room at this inn. I could go with the truth. *We were making out like high schoolers.* No. Nope. I'm not going to say that. They don't need to know, these nosy women that I've come to adore.

"What makes you think Noel was here?" I ask, because when trying to get someone off your trail, it's essential to give them reason to doubt. *Thank you, crime podcasts.* Also, denial seems like my best option right now.

Hattie comes over to the table. I didn't even know she was standing behind me. "The footprints in the snow leading up to that trellis under your window," she says, lifting her drawn-on eyebrows high on her forehead, a mischievous grin on her lips. "Wasn't hard to figure out."

Wow, I didn't give these two enough credit. I should have known, though. They're like old-lady supersleuths.

"Also," Irene says on a sigh, looking at her nails, "we have security cameras." She looks at me with a cheeky grin. "Noel installed them for us."

I let my mouth fall open. Noel? He installed security cameras? Why did he let me pretend to sneak him out the past two nights when he'd known there were cameras?

My eyes go wide as I think of the first night I snuck him out, after he climbed the trellis to my room. I got a little carried away kissing him goodbye and ended up with my legs wrapped around him as he held me. No wonder he kept trying to move us away from the door.

That's just great. I'd like to crawl into a hole now.

"Don't worry," says Hattie. "We deleted the security feed."

There's a feed? And they know how to access it?

I bury my face in my hands. "How much did you see?" I say through my fingers.

"Enough," says Irene.

I let out a long breath as I hear the chairs on both sides of me squeak and feel their presence as they each take a seat.

Irene puts a hand on my back. "We think you and Noel make a gorgeous couple."

I look up to see them both nodding their heads at me. My heart sinks into my gut, and I let out a long, sad sigh. "We can't be a couple," I say.

"Well, why not?" asks Irene.

"Because we live in different states."

"Oh, pishposh," says Hattie. "Those are just details."

"But they're kind of *big* details," I say.

"Do you love him?" asks Irene.

"What?" Do I love Noel? Is she seriously asking me this?

"I saw you two on the camera. It definitely looked like love," says Hattie, giving me a sly grin.

I cringe and it's a full-body one. Inside and outside. What Hattie saw was lust. It was not-thinking-of-the-consequences, over-the-top, thought-we-weren't-being-watched lust. And I just . . . I don't . . . Actually, the earth just needs to fall out from under me right now. Just suck me into a black hole, please.

I take a steadying breath. "I don't think I've known Noel long enough to call what we have 'love,'" I say.

"Oh"—Hattie waves my words away with her hand—"I knew I loved my Thomas from the moment I saw him. It was actual love at first sight."

"You did not," Irene argues. "You told me that he was a cocky, overconfident buffoon after you met him."

"No I didn't," protests Hattie.

"Yes, you did. We were in the backyard. You had on that little white dress, the one that you stole from me, and you . . ."

Here we go again. I slowly push back from my seat, as they're both leaning around me now, forgetting I'm even there, talking over each other and pointing, their faces starting to turn that same familiar shade of pink that's prevalent each and every time they argue.

I quietly get up from my chair and walk up the stairs to my room. They don't even notice. I can still hear them arguing as I go inside my room and shut the door.

I pick up my phone, flop onto my bed, and send a text to Cami.

Me: Feeling blue about never seeing Noel again after this

My phone chimes just a minute later.

Cami: Don't say that! Love conquers all!

I frown at my phone.

Me: I think I miss the old cynical you

She sends me back a winking emoji with its little tongue hanging out.

Cami: You really don't know what the future will hold

Me: Yes I do. Me in Carson City and him in Carole Cove. The end. Movie over.

I realize I haven't even told Cami about the land and my dad and the office thing. I haven't even had a chance to. And now I just feel like wallowing in my sorrow instead of celebrating.

Cami: No! It's not over. You can give this movie a happy ending. I have a good feeling about you two.

I scoff at my phone. This can't have a happy ending. I've already done the math. Besides, I don't want to remind Cami that once upon a time she had a good feeling about my brother and look where that got her.

I throw my phone down on the bed and look up at the ceiling, feeling like I want to scream. Or cry. Or scream-cry. I have too many thoughts and too many emotions running through me.

I need to get out of here and get some fresh air and maybe some caffeine. I throw on my coat and my Heathen Steven scarf, put on some boots, and leave my room. The sisters are still arguing as I walk down the grand staircase and out the door.

I breathe in the cold air as I make my way down Main Street, my hands in my pockets because I forgot gloves and it's ridiculously cold outside. I nuzzle into my scarf and realize I left in such a hurry that I forgot my earbuds and now I won't have any crime podcasts to keep me company. It's just as well. I need to think about life and not avoid it by listening to a detailed murder case.

I glance at the stores as I pass them, looking in windows and seeing people working and laughing. This stupid Christmas town. It's totally gotten under my skin. I don't even mind all the kitschy decor anymore. I kind of love it. It represents so much right now.

It doesn't take long before I'm standing in front of the Merry Little Coffee Shop. My heart does a little tugging thing and then sinks when I remind myself that Noel won't be inside. I open the door, and warm air and the smell of coffee wafts out. It doesn't change my mood.

Somehow, on the walk over here, I decided I'm angry. At my dad for making me come here, at Cami for encouraging me with Noel, and at myself for letting something happen with him when I knew better. At Irene and Hattie for watching me make out with Noel on their security footage. So much anger.

So, when I walk inside and see the Curmudgeonly Baker standing at the order station, her pointer finger jabbing in the air toward Ivy, and Ivy calmly taking it all, I snap.

I walk up to the counter and give the baker lady a very poignant look. "Excuse me," I say, looking at her directly.

"Yeah?" she says, looking down her nose at me. She's really got that look down. I'd be impressed if she weren't such a horrible person.

"I'm not sure what your end goal is here, but how about you just stop. Stop harassing this place, stop bothering Ivy. Go back to your bakery and do what you do best. Stop wasting her time," I say, gesturing toward a very wide-eyed Ivy. "And stop wasting your time." I gesture toward her.

"I'm *sorry*?" says the baker, her voice raspy, her nostrils flaring as a very distinct red color moves up her neck.

I push back my shoulders, not allowing myself to be intimidated by this woman. "Ivy's too nice to say this to your face, so I'll say it for her. Stop worrying about everyone else and go worry about yourself. You sell your goods; the coffee shop will sell theirs, which" —I hold out a hand at the protest I can tell she's about to make — "are not the same as yours and you know it."

The baker makes an exasperated huffing noise through her nose. She looks at Ivy; then she looks back at me. I glare at her with my I-mean-business stare. I've got my eyes opened wide and my mouth in a hard line.

I'm armed with more to say, but then without another word or protest, the rude baker lady turns on her heels and walks out the door, a blast of cold coming into the shop as she leaves.

I let out a very large exhale, dropping my shoulders as I do. "There," I say. I could have gone the cheesy holiday movie route and shown her love so she could see the real meaning of Christmas, but this was much more satisfying. I'll call this one *Mara Gives a Smackdown for Christmas*.

"Wow," Ivy says. "That was . . ."

"Sorry if I overstepped. It's been a morning, and I just couldn't take it anymore."

"Well done," Ivy says, looking at me with appraising eyes. "I should have said something a while ago."

"You did," I say. "She didn't listen. Sometimes it takes someone else saying something."

The bells on the door ring as someone walks in, and we both look over to see Pete walk in with Kaden. When he sees Ivy, Pete's eyes brighten almost as much as Kaden's.

"Mommy!" the little boy yells, as he runs over and gives her a hug. She hugs him back and then tells both him and Pete to go take a seat and she'll come over and sit with them in a second.

"What can I get you?" she asks, turning back to me.

"Actually," I say, looking over at Pete and Kaden and then back at Ivy. I think of what I just told her—*sometimes it takes someone else saying something.* Maybe that's what needs to happen here? Well, I'm in the mood to say it today, even if this is jumping way over boundaries. Here goes nothing.

I look at her. "You know those Christmas movies that we were talking about the other night at your family dinner?"

She nods, giving me a smile without teeth. I lean in toward her. "In a lot of those movies, the hero that the heroine ends up with is usually right under her nose."

Ivy gives me a confused look, her nose scrunched and her eyebrows pulled inward.

"Pete," I say, giving her wide please-understand-what-I'm-saying eyes.

"Pete?" She's still giving me a very questioning look.

"He's clearly crazy about you," I say, looking over my shoulder just in time to see Pete looking at Ivy, and then when he sees me catch him, he quickly looks away.

I turn back to Ivy, who's tucking her chin into her neck, her eyes growing wide. "Pete?"

"Yes," I say. "In this little holiday story, you're the heroine, and Pete is the hero."

"But . . ." She stops herself, looking over my shoulder at Pete and then back at me. "Pete's my friend. I've known him . . . forever."

"And doesn't that make the best kind of start to a relationship?"

"Pete . . . ," she says again. Like she's just taken a sip of wine and is letting it sit on her tongue as she tastes all the flavors.

I tilt my head to the side. "Honestly, has no one ever said this to you before?" She shakes her head. How is that possible? I'm sure people have seen it: the looks of longing from Pete, how they look like a family, the three of them spending all that time together. How has no one ever noticed? I'm feeling quite pleased with myself for saying something. The title of this movie would be *Mara the Amazing Christmas Matchmaker*. I may be getting ahead of myself.

"Pete," she says his name once more, this time her voice is almost a whisper.

"Of course, if you don't like him like that, then that makes sense," I offer, realizing it would take a mutual liking here for this to work.

"I've . . . never really thought of it," she says.

"Well, maybe consider it." I give her one little nod. "Also, I'd like a white-chocolate-and-peppermint latte, please."

Ivy punches my order in and takes my payment, all while in a bit of a fog. She acts like she's going to say something but then stops herself. She does this a few times, all while glancing at Pete and then at me and then back at Pete.

Okay, I've saved the town and told off the mean baker, and now Kaden might just have a dad soon enough — or at least the seed has been planted. I have no control over how that story will end. I'll just have to hope. Maybe I've been looking at this all wrong. Maybe the real happy ending of this story is for Ivy and Pete. Because I'm certainly not going to get one.

"So did you get everything done?" I ask Noel as we clean up the sitting area of the coffee shop after closing.

"All the paperwork is ready to go," Noel says as he lifts up a chair and turns it over, placing it on the table. He's putting all the chairs up so he can sweep and mop, and I'm helping.

We're all alone. The lighting in the shop is soft, the kind that everyone looks good in. The aroma of coffee still hangs in the air, and jazzy Christmas music plays in the background.

I went back to my room at the inn — after my meddling and fixing the town's problems earlier — to do some actual work, and then crocheted some of my hate away until Noel called to see if I wanted to meet him at the shop. Apparently, Ivy had asked him earlier if he could close up, saying she had something important to do this evening. I smiled when he told me. I hope it means good things.

I've already chastised him for the security camera thing and how embarrassing that was with the sisters. His reasoning for keeping me in the dark was not wanting to spoil all the fun I was having sneaking him out. He wasn't wrong about that. But it's all kind of tainted now. I'll never get to think back on how I practically attacked him as he was leaving without remembering that Irene and Hattie saw it. It's already making me feel sick.

I look around the shop. I'm going to miss this place. But not as much as I will miss the man who's currently trying to buff something out of a table with a rag. He looks over at me, catching me watching him, and he smiles, his dimples popping out to say hello.

We need to talk. I need to tell him all the things I was thinking about this morning. But I also don't want to. We're in a little bubble, the two of us together. And I don't know if I want to pop it just yet.

Like he can hear my thoughts, Noel ditches the rag and comes over to me as Nat King Cole starts singing about chestnuts roasting on an open fire.

He holds out a hand toward me. I take it, and wordlessly he pulls me into him, putting our clasped hands between us against his chest. He wraps his other arm around my waist as he begins rocking us back and forth to the melody.

I feel teary, all of a sudden, as he leans his cheek against mine and moves us in slow circles in the middle of the coffee shop. This is too much, and too hard. I thought I knew what I'd be risking by kissing Noel, but I didn't think it would be this.

This can't be the end. I don't want it to be. Cami's text from earlier pops into my head. *You can give this movie a happy ending.* Is it that simple? Am I giving up too easy? Isn't it worth trying?

I feel my heart beating in my chest as I pull my cheek away from Noel's so I can look him in the eyes.

I take a breath. "What are you doing for New Year's Eve?"

Noel stops the dancing and looks at me, his eyes searching my face. "What do you mean?"

"Well," I say, feeling suddenly buoyed up. My heart is racing and butterflies are multiplying in my chest, and the words are there, hanging on the tip of my tongue. "I'm going on that trip with Cami after I leave here. But I was just thinking, I don't have a date for New Year's Eve. And I thought, maybe it could be you." I swallow, all kinds of vulnerable feelings rushing through me.

"Yes," he says, not even skipping a beat, his eyes bright and sparkling under the overhead lighting. I can feel his heartbeat, my hand still in his, tucked against his chest. It's moving fast, matching mine. "Yes, please."

"I don't know about you, but I don't think I'm ready for this to end."

His head goes up and down in little rapid movements. "I've been racking my brain all morning trying to figure out how we can make this work."

"So have I," I say. "And I still don't have an answer, but . . . I want to try."

"Mara," he says. "I've never felt anything like I feel for you. I've been agonizing over saying goodbye to you the past couple of days."

I huff out a breath. At least I wasn't alone. We'd both been feeling the same way, then. "Me too," I say.

"I know," he says and then pauses. He takes in a wobbly breath. "I know this is probably too much, all these feelings I've been having. And I know it's probably too soon to say the l-word. But . . ." He stops talking, probably because of the wide-eyed look I'm giving him right now.

I swallow. "The l-word? You mean as in . . . liver?"

He shakes his head slowly. "Nope."

"Library?"

"Try again."

"Litigation?"

The corners of his mouth pull upward as he nods. "Yeah. That's the one. I think . . . I might litigation you."

I suck in a breath, my chest rising as I do. "I think I might litigation you too."

His lips are on mine, soft and sweet at first, but then morphing into something intense and heavy almost in an instant. He's released the hand that he was holding to his chest and is now cradling my face in both hands, angling my head so he can get better access.

I might agree with Cami. Despite everything, all the roadblocks, I think I have a good feeling about us too. And maybe this could be a happily ever after, after all.

∞∞∞∞∞∞

Later that night, or early the next morning—however you want to look at it—I walk Noel to the door of the inn and kiss him goodbye, inside this time. No need to be sneaky anymore or make out in the cold. That was fun while it lasted, though.

We didn't make plans just yet. We both decided that we need to just see what happens. There are a lot of hurdles for Noel and me. But at least we want to tackle them together.

I sort of drift back up to my room after he leaves. I'm feeling so light, so enamored with everything right now. Who knew when I arrived in this little town, I'd end up finding so much here.

I fall back onto my bed, with my phone in my hand, waiting for a text from Noel telling me he made it home so I can try to get at least a few hours of sleep.

I check my email while I wait, deleting a few ads and flagging some from clients to read later.

Then I see one that makes my throat drop into my stomach and my heart start to pound in my chest. It's clear as I read the words that it wasn't meant for me, yet I was cc'd. Whether by accident or on purpose, I'll probably never know.

I read the email once, twice, maybe a dozen times. The words won't change. No matter how I try to make sense of it.

There's no sense to be made — it's right there, glaring on the bright glow of my phone screen.

Everything has gone terribly wrong.

Chapter Seventeen

I only slept for maybe an hour. But it was fitful, and I look a bit like someone who was hit by a car this morning. My eyes are red, and there are bags for days. Oh, and I crocheted half a hat last night. It's black, as in the color of my dad's heart.

No amount of crocheting will be enough to fix the rage I have in my heart. And unfortunately, it can't change what he's done.

I read the email again. Just in case something has changed since the last hundred times I've read it.

> **To:** ToddGMoody@Mericardservices.com
> **CC:** JayScott@Scottfamilyrealty.com,
> MaraScott@Scottfamilyrealty.com
> **From:** ShannonHill@Scottfamilyrealty.com
> **RE:** Land in Montana

Todd,

I'm happy to inform you that Jay was able to secure the land in Carole Cove, MT. The contract will be signed on Saturday. He told me to tell you the build-out can start in early spring, weather permitting.

Scott Realty is happy we found a new campus for the MeriCard headquarters. We look forward to working with you on this development.

Best,
Shannon Hill
Assistant to Jay Scott

Nope, the words are the same. I've read it so many times, I think I have it memorized.

He lied to me. My dad *lied* to me. This was never about buying land for our family like he said. It was only about him and lining *his* pockets. And I did all his dirty work without even knowing. He planned this. He wanted me to think we were doing something good, he knew that I wouldn't be willing to do something this devious. So he made me think . . . he made me believe . . .

I pick up my phone to call him once again. I've probably tried fifty times, each call going straight to voice mail. I continue calling because he has some explaining to do. I keep hoping he's playing a big trick on me. But that doesn't really make any sense. Plus, it would go against everything I know about my dad. He's never been a joker. A lying, cheating, jerk, yes. Someone who likes to play practical jokes, never.

I tried my mom—as soon as it was a decent enough time to call—to find out if she knew where he was. She had no idea, of course. She's still in the west wing of the house and not speaking to him. I didn't have the time or desire to explain to her why I needed to talk to him so desperately. It didn't matter—she was only interested in telling me that Claudia and Ben are separated. Cue the pretend shock.

"You've reached Jay Scott . . . ," I hear in my ear and hang up. I've already left him a dozen threatening emails and texts. He's been known to turn off his phone for hours at a time, but I'm surprised he has it turned off today with the sale happening soon.

Well, he can find out later that there was no sale today, because it's *not* happening. My dad may think he's bested me, but I'm the one here finalizing contracts. I'm the one who has to sign everything. And little old naive me would have fully done it had I not seen that email. But now I won't be taking part in his dirty work. I won't be signing any contracts or helping with anything that will ruin this town.

I'll go to the auction this morning—in just over an hour—and I'll tell them. I'll tell the mayor and Noel that they can't go through with this sale to my dad and that they have to go through with the auction. I can't save this town from whoever will win, but I can save it from my dad.

If it ruins my chance at running the office in Carson City, then so be it. I'm not sure I want a future working for a man who's so low, so ruthless, as to use his own daughter to get what he wants.

The sad part is, this isn't the first time he's done this. Not on this scale, but I've done work for him before that didn't sit quite right with me. Using already-sold listings to bring in new clients with the promise we can find them something better, steering potential clients to our own listings to make double the profit on the sale and the purchase, not showing properties that won't get us a big enough cut. All these things are common practice in this business—unethical, but not illegal. And I did them because he asked me to, until I fully understood what I was doing. Once I found out, I told him I wouldn't do it again and I've stood by my word.

How did I not figure out he was up to something with this sale? How did I not see through him? I know why: because no one wants to believe their parent is an actual jerkface, even if there's so much evidence to prove it. But if he looks like a jerkface, talks like a jerkface, does business like a jerkface, chances are . . . he's a jerkface.

I feel like such an idiot. And now the future of this town—a town that I've kind of grown to adore—is up in the air again.

But . . . is it? As I'm splashing cold water on my face to try and help my skin not look so sallow, a thought comes to me and takes flight so quickly, it's like a ton of info coming at me all at once, as if my brain is shouting at me. The idea is far-fetched and would take a miracle. But I have to try. It's kind of my only hope.

I get dressed frantically, putting my shirt on backward not once, but twice, and throwing on my coat, boots, and scarf. I run down the stairs so quickly and so loudly, the noise scares both Hattie and Irene.

"Do either of you know where I can find David Bersham?" I've never been more grateful to be staying with the town gossips than I am right now. If anyone will know where he is, it's these two.

Hattie, with a hand on her heart trying to calm herself, gives me a confused look. "Why would you want to find him?"

"It's a long story, but I need to talk to him."

"You look just awful," says Irene, who seems to have recovered from my accidental scare quicker than Hattie. "Have you been crying?"

Hattie's confused look turns to concerned. "You do look like you've been crying. Did you and Noel have a fight?"

"I'm sure whatever was said, you two can work it out," says Irene.

"No." I shake my head. I'm feeling frantic now, I have so little time. "I couldn't sleep . . ."

"Is it an incompatibility thing? Like," Irene cuts me off, her head angled to the side as she examines me. Her drawn-on eyebrows move up her forehead. "A between-the-sheets problem?" She lowers her voice to a whisper when she says this, even though it's just us three in the front room.

"What? Oh my gosh, no," I say, shaking my head in rapid movements.

Hattie's got the same look now. "Oh yes, that can be a problem with new couples." She gives me an understanding look, like she has it all figured out. "It's important to learn what your partner likes. I've got a book you should read. With my Thomas, I never wanted to—"

"PLEASE!" I say loudly, making them both jump. I really don't want her to finish that sentence. "Noel and I aren't fighting. We're fine."

I hope we are, at least. Maybe after today, after learning what kind of person I'm related to, Noel might second-guess his feelings. I know in my gut that's not the kind of person he is, but the worry makes my stomach sink nonetheless. I can't entertain this thought train right now, though. I need to hurry.

"Can either of you tell me where I can find David Bersham? Is he at home around this time? Do you have an address?"

Irene gives me a quizzical look. "I can tell you where he lives, but he's been seen at the Jolly Café a lot recently. I bet he's there. Probably can't show his face back at Noel's coffee shop, after what happened. They got in a fight, you know."

"Yes, yes," I say as I run to the door, hoping and praying that I can find David in time. "Thank you!"

I run over to the Jolly Café, go inside, and walk right by Sammy the hostess and into the dining area, where I scan the room. It would make things so much easier if he were here. I need this one thing to go right today.

The universe is conspiring on my side, apparently, because he's here, sitting over in the corner, a cup of coffee on the table in front of him. He's looking at nothing in particular, just staring off like he did at the coffee shop.

I don't hesitate. I walk over to him and stand by his table. "Hi, Mr. Bersham. I'm Mara Scott."

"Yes?" He looks up at me; his salt-and-pepper mustache has been neatly groomed.

"May I?" I point to the chair across from him, and he gives me a dip of his chin.

"What can I do for you?" he asks after I take a seat. He has kind eyes. I'm sort of taken aback by them, having never seen them up close. There's a story there, I can tell. And it goes against everything I've been told about this man, everything I've seen.

"I need to ask you about the land that's going to auction today."

He furrows his brow. "What about it?"

"I know you pulled out of the bid, but . . ." I stop to take a breath and try to organize my words in the way I want to say them. "Well, I've heard rumors about what you wanted to do with it—the land—and I just wanted to know what your plan was."

I feel butterflies swim around in my belly. This feels like such a long shot, I'm not even sure it's worth taking. But I have to do something. I have to try.

David's eyes move toward the window. "It's not important," he says. "I'm not going to bid on the land."

"Do you not want it anymore?"

He shakes his head, slowly. "I still want it, but in order to keep the peace around here, it's best if I let it go. This town will go down in ashes, and I can do nothing about it but watch."

He looks pained when he says this, like it physically hurts him to think about it.

I take a breath and then lick my dry lips. "Was your plan really to push the town as a summer getaway?"

He tilts his head to the side, probably wondering how I— someone who's not from this town, a person he's never actually met—would know this.

"That was my plan, yes," he says.

"What did you want to do?"

He hesitates for only a second before he begins detailing his plan to me. Cabins on the property by the road, which could be used for a variety of activities—family reunions, camping groups, romantic getaways for couples. A boathouse on the property by the lake where paddleboats and canoes could be rented in the summer and when the lake fully freezes over in mid-January, skating and ice fishing.

I listen to his ideas, my mind spinning as he talks. There's so much potential there, I'm surprised no one has done it before. Why can't people get on board with this?

"No one wants to change the Christmas town we've been selling for decades, because that's what we're known for," David says when I ask him why.

"But can't you still be a Christmas town in the summer too?"

He points a finger at me, acknowledging that I understand where he's coming from. "Yes. That's what I told the town council. But they didn't like the idea; or really, Chris didn't. In the past we've had so much tourism around the holidays, we didn't need to keep it going in the summer. But things have changed."

I give him an incline of my head, understanding. "I was told your plan would cost the city money and that was the real problem."

He shakes his head. "That's not true. I've got the funds, and funding lined up for the entire project."

"Then why would they think that?"

He lets out a breath. "Christopher Holiday has his beliefs."

"Oh," I say, seeing the full picture now. Pride, again. It almost always comes back to that when people are fighting.

"I don't understand how he can't let something go that happened such a long time ago."

I bob my head, remembering what Ivy told me about the land deal from so long ago. The one where David basically screwed over Christopher.

"I made mistakes when I was younger. I know I did," he continues without me having to ask. "I own those mistakes. Hell, I even tried to make it right, tried to give Chris money." David looks out the window at the nearly empty Main Street. "But he wouldn't have it. Wouldn't take help from me. And now, when I've got the capital to help save this place, he doesn't trust me. Prideful old man."

I take a big breath. "What if there's a chance to get you that land?"

He scrunches his brow again. "How?"

"I have an idea. But first, let me ask you this," I say. "Do you have the funds to pay for the land in cash right now?"

He looks at me like he's not sure he wants to answer this.

"Please, Mr. Bersham. I know you don't know me, but I promise you can trust me."

He gives me one simple nod. "I can pay cash for the lot."

"Okay," I say on an exhale. "If you can come to the auction with me, we might have a chance. No guarantees, but we have to try."

"Why?" he asks me, his face concerned. "Why do you want to do this?"

I don't have time to spell it all out for him, so I just say, "Because I want this town to survive too."

Chapter Eighteen

After answering a few more of his questions, I leave the Jolly Café with David Bersham, and we make our way to the town center building.

I'm feeling all sorts of feelings right now. Anxious, worried, a little pukey. There are so many things that could go wrong with my plan, number one being that Mayor Holiday hates the man who holds the keys that might make everything right. The town gets the money for the sale and tax revenue from it as well. If they can build the summer tourism, then it might just get this place back to thriving again.

The room is already pretty full, with Mayor Holiday and some of the town council sitting at the front. There's also the same guy from the county. All of them seated and ready.

And Noel's there. He's in a suit again, this time light gray, with a navy-blue tie. He's so handsome, and my heart does a leaping thing when I see him. Like he can sense my presence, his eyes turn toward me. The anxiety I'm feeling right now must be apparent, because he gives me a worried look.

I try to give him a reassuring smile. Then I take a breath, push my shoulders back, and walk to the table where the mayor is sitting, David following a few steps behind me.

The mayor's face drops when he sees the two of us. "What are you doing here, David?" he says, his voice loud over the low rumble of the room, his seething resentment for the man I've brought with me written all over his face.

"Mayor Holiday," I say, pulling David by his coat so he's standing next to me. We need to be a united front. "I need to speak with you before you start the meeting."

"What about?" The mayor gives me a questioning glance. He looks to David, and then his eyes travel to a spot just behind me.

I'm about to turn and see where his eyes went, but then I hear it. A deep, quiet-but-powerful voice I've known my whole life. "Hello, Mara."

I freeze in my spot, my eyes widening. I turn slowly around and see him. My dad, sitting in the front row in a black tailored suit and a long black wool coat. His mouth is quirked up on one side, his brows pulled down. In my head I hear that three-note sound when a movie takes a turn for the worse. *Dun, dun, duuuunnnn.*

"Dad?" I say.

I look to his left to see Michael, wearing nearly the same thing and looking like his little crony, as they both sit there with their legs casually crossed in the same manner.

"Why are you here?" I ask him.

"I came here to help you, of course," my dad says, one of his signature schmoozing grins on his face. "Flew in last night, thought I would surprise you."

This is a lie. Jay Scott doesn't do surprises. He couldn't have known about the email. I got it last night. So that means he came out here to make sure this sale happens. He must have a lot riding on this land purchase. *Well, too bad for him.*

I have so much I need to say, and when I open my mouth to do so, I hear the man from the county: "Attention, everyone."

Right. I need to remember where I am. I need to hold it together. My dad's here, and so what? Nothing's been done yet. We have steps to follow here. The auction will be canceled, and then the paperwork for the land will be signed. I wanted to talk to the mayor beforehand, but maybe this is the better way. After the auction is canceled and my dad has been outed, David Bersham will be the only option for the town. The mayor won't have a choice. This could be the universe pulling for me again. I can only hope.

I look to David, who's standing by me with a curious look on his face. Once again, there's too much to explain, so I just give him a reassuring nod, like everything is going to plan, and we move to the side of the room so we don't block anyone's view.

"Listen up, everyone," the man from the county says. "We're sorry to inform you all that as of nine thirty this morning, we have come to an agreement with a buyer and the lot has been sold. Therefore, the auction is canceled. We thank you for your time."

Wait. What? What did he just say? Sold? I couldn't have heard him right.

"What do you mean?" I say aloud, but no one can hear me as the volume of the room grows louder with frustrated people voicing their anger over having had to come out here twice, only for the auction to be canceled.

Some of the people are complaining to each other, some loudly enough that they can be heard over the din of the room. I watch as everyone angrily starts to file out until all that's left is Noel and the mayor, my dad and Michael, and David and me.

"Did he say it was sold?" David asks me.

"I . . . I'm not sure," I say.

Holding out hope the guy from the county has it wrong, I walk over to the table where the mayor is, David following me.

"Mayor Holiday," I say as we approach. "What did he mean—that man from the county—about the land being sold? I thought that was happening after you canceled the auction."

Mayor Holiday stands up, first giving David a very crap-eating grin, and then he turns to me, his smug look morphing into a happy one. "Your father—wonderful man by the way—met up with us before the meeting. Everything's done," he says, reaching up and adjusting his red bow tie. "All signed." He then taps two fingers on a thick white contract folder on the table in front of him.

"It's been signed?" I ask, hoping I heard wrong.

"Yes," he says, delighted. "And all thanks to you." He gives me a wink, and I feel the blood rush from my face.

"Mara?" Noel says with a worried look on his face, coming to stand by his dad, the plastic table between us. "Are you okay? What's wrong?"

I shake my head, feeling like I might be sick. *This can't be happening.*

"Can it be unsigned?" I frantically ask Noel and his dad, who are both giving me concerned looks. "Were there any clauses in there? Contingencies?"

Noel shakes his head. "It's a solid contract. I went over it myself. What's going on, Mara?"

I look to David, who gives me a sad, resigned look, and then he heads toward the exit. My wild card, no longer an option. It's just as well. I can't fix this—contracts are for buyers, not sellers. How many times have I dealt with a seller who decided they wanted out of a contract? Unless there are clauses or contingencies built in to protect them up front, they rarely have a leg to stand on once the contract is signed.

"No, no, no," I say, putting my face in my hands.

"Mara?" Noel says, his voice worried.

I can't look at him. I can't look him or his dad in the eyes and tell them what I need to tell them next.

But I don't have to, because my dad starts talking. "I think Mara is overwhelmed," he says. "She doesn't know how to tell you that Carole Cove is the new home of MeriCard."

"What?" I hear the mayor say. "Mara?"

I pull my hands away from my face and look up at the shocked and confused faces of Noel and his dad. The fluid gathering in the base of my eyelids fills to the brim, and tears begin to topple over and down my face, down my cheeks, and to my neck.

"I . . . didn't know," I say on a sob.

"Of course, you did," my dad says. I feel him standing next to me, but I won't look at him—I can't. He puts an arm around my shoulders. "Of course, Mara knew. This was our plan, after all."

"No, it wasn't," I say, looking at my father like I hardly know him. But I do know him, and this was never about me and about the office in Carson City. This was about him and his money. He doesn't even deserve one of my rage scarves.

"Mara did exactly what I asked her to do," my dad says, in that quiet but intense voice of his.

"You said the land was for posterity," I say, my eyes wide.

"Are you serious right now?" Noel says to my dad, his nostrils flaring, a deep shade of crimson climbing up his face. "The land we just sold you is going to MeriCard?" He curses under his breath when my dad nods his head. So, this is Noel when he's mad.

The mayor shakes his head and closes his eyes. He opens them on my dad. "You tricked us," he says. "You sent your daughter"—he points an index finger at me—"to trick us into selling you this land."

"I didn't trick you," my dad says, keeping his cool. I've never seen him lose it. Not even with my mom. It's all meant to manipulate. All to keep the upper hand.

"You just didn't tell us the whole truth," Noel says. He looks from my dad to me.

"I didn't know," I say again, trying to plead my case. It seems to be the only thing I can say, my only defense.

"You're a despicable human. Both you and your daughter." For a second, I think the mayor is going to punch my dad, just like David Bersham. I kind of wish he would.

"Hey now," says Michael, coming over to us and taking a stance near my dad like he'd protect him. Which is laughable. My dad is much bigger than Michael.

The mayor breathes out his nose, like he's trying to calm himself. Then he picks up the folder with the contract in it and shakes it at my dad. "We'll fight this," he says.

My dad just dips his head once, like he was expecting this response.

"Come on, Noel," the mayor says, walking toward the exit.

"Mara," my dad says after a few beats. "Let's go." He walks toward the exit, too, Michael with him.

And then it's just me and Noel. Standing there with a crappy plastic folding table between us.

"I . . . ," I say on a sob. "I didn't . . ." I close my eyes, tears pouring out of them in rapid succession.

"Know," he says, finishing my sentence. My only line.

"My dad . . . he . . . he used me." There. More words.

Noel lets out a breath. And then gives me a sad, resigned smile. For a moment it seems like he wants to reach out to me, to take me in his arms. But he doesn't. He gives me one last look, shakes his head, and walks out of the room.

I cry for a few minutes in the now-quiet town center building. All by myself, just me and my sobs, a fluorescent light flickering above me.

I've ruined everything. I know if Cami were here, she'd tell me it wasn't my fault, but it kind of is. I should have known; I should have read between the lines. Why did I blindly believe my dad wanted to sit on some land? How foolish that all sounds to me now.

My blood boils, and acid builds in my gut as I walk out of the town building.

"Dad," I say when I see him standing by Michael's Porsche, talking to him.

He doesn't say anything when he hears me; he just lets out an exhale, his warm breath making a cloud in the cold air. The skies are overcast, and snow is starting to fall. Instead of the cozy, cuddle-up-with-a-blanket kind of feeling I usually get on a day like this, it just feels ominous and foreboding.

My dad gives Michael a quick incline of his head, his facial expression saying, *Leave us alone for a minute,* and Michael opens his car door and gets in.

"How could you?" I say, lighting into him. He doesn't say anything. He just looks at me. "You lied to me."

He shakes his head. "No, I didn't."

"You told me that you wanted that land for posterity . . . for our family," I say.

"Yes, this property is going to make our family a lot of money," he says. "It's the start of big things for Scott Realty."

I shake my head. "No," I say on a sob. "You said you were going to sit on it. You led me to believe . . . ," I cut off, trying to think of all the things he said to me. Had he only said he wanted it for posterity? Did he ever tell me he was just going to sit on it? Or was that something I made up?

He shakes his head. "I never said those things."

"But you never told me," I say.

"You never asked."

"But you let me believe it. You made me come here and get these people to trust me, to believe in me." I hiccup from all the crying. "You used me."

"I'm sorry you feel that way," he says.

I shake a finger at him. "No, don't try to manipulate me, like you do with everyone else. Like you do with Mom."

"Mara," he says and then drops his hands by his side. "What do you want me to say to you?"

"I want you to admit you used me. I want you to apologize. And if you've ever loved me a day in your life, then you will pull out of that contract."

"Mara," he says again, his head tilted to the side. "I can't do that."

I take a tentative step toward him. "Yes, you can. For me. Because it's the right thing to do." I look into his hazel eyes, the ones he gave me. "Do the right thing for me."

He looks at me, and then at the sky, and then the ground beneath his feet. He takes in a big inhale. "I'm sorry, Mara. My hands are tied."

I let my shoulders drop. He won't do the right thing. I don't know if Jay Scott has ever done the right thing in his entire career. He's only done the thing that serves him best.

"I don't want the office in Carson City," I say. "I quit."

"Come on, Mara," he says. "You don't really want to do that."

"Yes, I do," I say. And then I turn and walk toward the inn.

Chapter Nineteen

I lock myself in my room for the rest of the day after walking away from my dad. He called me a couple of times and sent me a text asking if we could talk. But I didn't respond. Right now I'm not sure I ever want to talk to him again. He might be the new recipient of the "Don't answer this call" listing in my phone. *Step aside, Heathen Steven, there's a new a-hole in town.*

My head is pounding and my nose is raw, and every once in a while, I let out a little hiccup from all the crying I've done. I can't remember the last time I cried like this. It's been a long time, though. I tend to get angry more than sad. But I have so much to be sad about right now. I've let so many people down.

I send Noel a text after a couple of hours, asking him if we can talk, so I can explain. But he doesn't respond. He probably needs space — maybe it will be a day, or maybe it will be forever. It's not like we can make this work now. There can't be a happy ending. Even if we tried, every time he looked at me, he'd remember what happened — even if I was just an unsuspecting victim in my dad's grand scheme. And even if he could overlook all that, what about my guilt? I don't think I can ever get over it.

Around three in the afternoon, I decide to get over my pity party and tell myself that it's time to take action. I've got to fix this. I'll stay in this town as long as I have to. However long they'll let me. So far, I haven't gotten an eviction notice from Hattie and Irene. They've actually been very sweet, bringing food to my room and leaving it by the door. I'm sure they'll kick me to the curb once they find out what I did. But, if and when that happens, I'll drive to a neighboring town and stay there, or I'll sleep in my tin rental car. I will make this right before I leave.

In order to do that I need to tell Cami something she's not going to want to hear. I don't have time to explain what happened. Not right now. Besides, what would I say? *Turns out I'm the villain of this movie.*

I send her a text.

Me: I'm so sorry, Cam. I have to cancel the Virgin Islands. Things are a mess here. I'll explain more later. I hope you still love me.

She responds almost immediately.

Cami: Of course I love you! The Virgin Islands will always be there. We can go another time. I hope everything is okay. Call when you can.

I take a big cleansing breath, feeling grateful to at least have Cami, who will always love me no matter what.

"All right, Ollie," I say to the ostrich sitting in the chair by the window. "We've got work to do."

I work tirelessly for hours, researching anything I can find online, leaving messages for contract attorneys who might be willing to talk with me. I work my way through the type of contract that was used for the sale, looking for whatever jumps out at me, hoping I can find something.

I go through zoning requirements, usage restrictions, flooding possibilities for the land, anything and everything that could be a loophole. I even spend a ridiculous amount of time researching endangered species in the area — plants or animals — wondering if, somehow, I could trap them and rehome them on the lot. I'm not sure how I'd find any black-footed ferrets in the area, but I'm willing to try if it's my only option.

By ten at night, my eyes are crossed and I feel like I'm not making any headway. I haven't found anything substantial to help the town. Only confirmation that unless the buyer agrees to some sort of payout — which I'm sure isn't on the table as far as my dad's concerned — or they're willing to walk away from the contract, there's not much that can be done.

I fall back on my bed faceup, looking at the popcorn ceiling. It all feels like a lost cause. There's only one way out of this and it's never going to happen. I sit up and pull my computer onto my lap and send my dad an email anyway. I could call him, but I know I'll get heated and then my words won't come out like I need them to.

Dad,

I know I asked you this last night, but I need you to hear it again. Please, stop the sale. This town, it means something to me. I didn't like it when I first got here, but then somehow, it got under my skin.

The people here, how they help each other, how they take pride in what they have is inspiring. They take care of one another. I've never been in a place like this before, or around people like this, and bringing in a big corporation like MeriCard . . . well, that will ruin everything they have, everything they've worked for.

I know the town means nothing to you because you've never been here except for those few hours today. So you have no ties to it. But I do. And I know I've asked you for many things in my life, but had I known this would be in my future, I would have taken them all back if it meant you would do this one thing for me.

There are plenty of other towns for MeriCard. Ones that would even welcome them, I bet. I will help you scour the nation to find one if you will please help me save this place.

–Mara

I take a big breath as I hit send.

I lie back down on my bed and feel tears fall down from the corners of my eyes and into my hair. They just come of their own accord now. I don't even fight it.

Just as I'm starting to spiral down to my pity party again, I hear a noise. Something has hit my window. Something that sounds very much like the noise from the night Noel climbed up the trellis and kissed me like I was the only person he'd ever want to kiss for the rest of his life.

I'm thinking it's a fluke, but then I hear it again.

I scramble up from my bed and clumsily go to the window, practically tripping over my own feet. I don't peek out or worry there's a serial killer. I open the window and stick my head out.

And there he is. Noel. Standing near the lamppost once again.

"Hey," I say, feeling those pesky tears prickle behind my eyes.

"Hi," he says, giving me a little wave. I can't see his face very well in the dark, but there's definitely no smiling happening right now.

"What are you doing?" he asks, in that same stage whisper he used a few nights ago. Back when everything felt so right in my world.

"Oh, . . . you know. Just canceling trips to the Virgin Islands and trying to save a town."

He dips his head once, and I think I see a smile. Maybe? Or did I just make it up in my head?

"You canceled your trip?"

"I did," I say.

"Can I come up?"

I'm interrupted by the squeaking noise of another window being opened somewhere below mine. I look and see a head pop out. Then another head pops out. Pink and gray hair glowing in the Christmas lights.

"Some of us are trying to sleep, you know," says Irene.

"Just come inside, Noel," says Hattie. "And use the front door this time, not the trellis. If you break your neck, so help me."

"Oh, and make this girl eat something," Irene says, pointing a thumb toward me. "She's been starving herself up there."

"Okay," Noel says to them. He gives them a little head bob and then turns and jogs toward the entrance.

It's only a matter of seconds before I hear the soft tap on my door. I open it, and there he is. In a black coat, dark jeans, and a navy-blue sweater. The sight of him makes my heart leap and my insides churn. A mixture of happy and sad.

"I'm—" I start, but then the tears choke me up and I can't talk.

He comes in and shuts the door behind him. He stands there, not sure what to do with his hands. I wonder if he wants to reach out for me like I want him to. But I think that might be all one sided, especially when his eyes look down at the floor. It's probably hard for him to make eye contact with me. The person who ruined everything, even if I didn't know I was doing it.

I swallow and take a steadying breath. "I'm sorry, Noel. I had no idea."

He jerks his head up, his eyes coming to mine. "I know," he says. "I know you wouldn't do that."

"You do?"

"Of course," he says. "I haven't known you all that long, but I *know* you, Mara. You wouldn't do something like that. I . . ." He stops himself, looking at his hands. "I was upset, earlier today—at the auction. And I needed to think."

I nod my head in little, tiny rapid movements. It makes my head spin a bit, with how stuffy I am from all the crying.

"Did you figure anything out?"

"About the land?"

I nod again.

"No," he says, a sad smile on his face. "I've looked at everything, thought of everything. Turns out I suck as a lawyer. Or maybe I was too good when I helped put that contract together. Did you . . . find anything?"

I shake my head, and I see the flicker of hope that was briefly on his face burn out, replaced by a solemn downturn of his lips.

"Not unless you know how to trap black-footed ferrets and get them to set up camp on the lot."

He scrunches his brow. "What?"

"Yeah . . . it's . . . never mind," I say, waving the dumb joke away with my hands. He lets out a chuckle anyway.

"David Bersham came to talk to me, at the coffee shop," Noel says, after a few beats of silence.

My eyes widen at that. "He did? And you . . . talked to him?"

"Yeah. He told me you came to see him this morning."

"A whole lot of good that did," I say.

"I listened to his plan."

"You did?"

He nods once. "I put all the family drama and all the rumors aside."

"What did you think?"

"It's a good plan," he says. "It would have been the best one for the town. If only my dad had just listened. If he'd have just gotten over himself. But . . ."

"But it's too late," I say. "Because of me." The tears threaten to emerge again.

He puts a hand out this time, resting it on my arm and then letting it slide down to my hand, where he wraps his fingers around mine. My heart starts picking up its pace with the contact. "I know you didn't do this, Mara."

"But my dad did. And I helped him."

"You . . ."

"Didn't know," I finish. We both smile and I huff out a laugh, remembering earlier today when that was pretty much all I could say.

He looks at me, his gaze turning more serious. He tentatively places his other hand, the one that wasn't holding mine, on my waist, just above my hip, and I take in a quick breath when he guides me toward him.

"I talked to Ivy," he says, his eyes on mine.

"Yeah?" I ask.

"I guess I have you to thank for her and Pete."

My eyebrows shoot up. And then I smile and chuckle. So, there is a happily ever after in this movie, after all. "Well, something needed to be said. I hope it's not weird for you . . . having your other best friend in love with your sister."

He chuckles this time. That low, rumbling one that makes me lean into him. "Yeah, it's weird," he says. "But . . . it makes sense too. She's . . . happy, happier than I've seen her in a long time. And Pete too. I think Kyle would be good with it. It all kind of makes sense. I don't know why I didn't see it before."

"Because she's your sister," I say. "And the situation is complicated."

He leans in and touches his forehead to mine. "Things just got a whole lot more complicated for us, didn't they?"

"Yeah," I say, feeling my heart land at the bottom of my stomach. I've thought of all the scenarios — when I'd allowed myself to hold out hope — and no matter how I tried, nothing ended with a happily ever after for Noel and me. It was already complicated enough without this.

He pulls his head back from mine, searching my eyes. "We could try, though? Couldn't we?"

I fall even harder for him with those words. After all this, he wants to try? Most men, at least the ones I've had relationships with, take the easy road whenever they can. Even my own father, who's currently taking the easiest road possible. The easiest and the most lucrative.

I put a hand on Noel's chest, feeling his heartbeat beneath it. I could tell him that I quit my job, that I'm now free to go wherever I want. Maybe I could ask him to run away to Alaska and start a new life with me. Or actually, Hawaii sounds like a better fantasy. We could be beach bums together, learn how to surf.

But I can't tell him that. It would only make things worse. The hard truth is, I can't make a life with Noel. Not here at least. And he has too much to lose if he leaves, with his family here, and his house, and the shop.

If I stayed, how would that work? I'd have to watch as MeriCard moves in and changes the whole dynamic of this town. I don't know if I'd be able to forgive myself with the constant reminders. And even if I got over that, would anybody besides Noel want me here? The secret would get out for sure this time. I've seen how this town has treated David Bersham, and he's been a member of this community for decades. I'd always be known as the woman who brought big business to Carole Cove.

Relationships are hard as it is, and this one has too many roadblocks, too many complications and unknowns plaguing it from the very beginning. Most of which can—and probably will—lead to resentment down the road, from both of us. Then I'd find myself in a relationship like my parents'. And I definitely don't want that.

The tears are back, running down my cheeks now. I don't like it. I know how to handle angry Mara. But this sobbing mess is foreign to me.

I do the hard thing and take a step back, away from him, so we aren't so close. So I can't smell his spicy scent or feel his breath on my face. The hand that was at my waist drops to his side. But he leaves his other one entangled with mine, neither of us able to completely let go.

"I don't think so, Noel," I say. "Things were verging on impossible before. And now . . ."

"I get it," he says. "I've been running through all the scenarios in my mind."

"So have I."

He gives me a sad smile, maybe the saddest one I've ever seen on his face.

"I think we need to look at this for what it is," I say, attempting to be strong. "Two people living two different lives, and no amount of litigation can make it work."

We both chuckle at that. It lightens the mood a bit.

"So not a litigation-conquers-all thing, then," he says. I think he meant it as a joke, but the serious look on his face says otherwise.

I shake my head slowly. "I wish things were different."

"Me too."

I look down, feeling Noel's thumb running back and forth over my hand. "I guess this is goodbye, then," I say, not able to look him in the eyes when I say it because I know my fragile heart will crack and break into a million pieces if I do.

"I guess so," he says.

I risk a glance at him and see the sheen in his eyes. Then I lean in and touch my lips to his. I need to feel them one last time. He kisses me back. It's longer than a peck but nothing like the kisses I really want from him. I'm pretty sure I could melt into him right now and we could make out, right here. One last time. But I pull my lips away too soon. It will only make this harder.

He takes in a deep breath, like he'd forgotten how to do it. He gives me a smile. It doesn't reach his eyes, not a dimple in sight. So many words left unsaid in the upturn of his lips. I feel them all.

"Goodbye, Noel," I say.

"Goodbye, Mara."

He gives me one last look, and then he opens the door to my room and leaves.

Chapter Twenty

The next morning, I'm sitting on my suitcase, trying to get it to shut again. It's even more full because of the things I purchased while I was here—the souvenirs and the yarn. Honestly, I'm starting to wonder why anyone would need as many coats as I seem to own. But somehow, probably by divine intervention, I'm able to zip up the hard case.

I'm going home today. The sun is shining, and the airport in Missoula has finally been dug out. I know I said I was going to stay here until I fixed this, but there's nothing that can be fixed. I never heard from my dad, which was essentially my only hope. So my only choice is to return home to Carson City and figure out my next move.

Turns out I could have gone to the Virgin Islands with Cami after all. I thought about calling her and telling her, but I don't think I want to sit on a beach and drink piña coladas. It all just feels so tainted now. *Sorry, Carole Cove. MeriCard is moving in and ruining your little town. I tried to save you, but I couldn't. So off to the beach I go!*

I look out the window and watch as the little Christmas town, that now means so much to me, comes to life as the stores start to open their doors. Some store owners are outside, wiping down windows and removing icicles from awnings. I watch as Sammy from the Jolly Café puts an A-frame sign outside the door where I first got to know Noel.

I don't think anyone knows quite yet that their lives are about to change with MeriCard. Maybe it will be for the better? Who knows? It doesn't seem like it will, but I can hope.

I put on my cream coat with the black buttons, tie my Heathen Steven scarf around my neck, and take one last look at the room that's been my home for almost two weeks. I give Ollie a little wave as I walk out the door and shut it behind me.

I take my stuff downstairs and set it all by the front door. Both sisters are in the front room—Hattie cleaning, and Irene looks to be rehanging some mistletoe.

"A little breakfast before you go?" asks Hattie, who's currently wiping down a table.

"I'm good," I say, but then put a finger to my chin. "Well . . . maybe I could take a couple biscuits for the road."

Hattie lifts a chin toward the console table by the door. I look and see a white box tied with a red ribbon and garnished with mistletoe. On top of it is a jar of what I can only hope is that amazing raspberry-peach jam.

"For me?"

"Of course," Hattie says, abandoning the rag on the table and walking toward me, Irene right behind her.

"We're going to miss you," she says, pulling me into a hug.

I hug her tight and then do the same with Irene. I blink away stupid tears.

After releasing Irene, I walk over to my purse. "I have something for you," I say.

I pull out the two scarves I made: a black one and the one in chartreuse. They both turned out prettier than I expected, and since my dad doesn't deserve anything from me, I knew who the rightful owners should be. I hand them each one.

"Oh," says Hattie, putting hers around her neck. "How lovely."

"Thank you, dear," says Irene.

I put my purse over my shoulder, and then, pulling the telescoping handle out of my suitcase, I grab onto it and lean it on its wheels, ready to leave.

"I guess I better go."

"Roads are clear today," says Irene.

"You drive safe, even so," says Hattie.

I can only smile and nod at the pair. I will really miss them.

I give them a little wave, and then open the door, not ready to leave this place but knowing that I must.

I run right into someone. I look up to find Noel. He seems out of breath, his cheeks and nose red from the cold.

"Noel?"

"Oh good," he says, through heavy breathing. "You haven't left yet."

I search his face. "I'm just heading out now." I look down at the suitcase in my hand as proof.

"You can't go," he says.

I start to shake my head. "Noel. Don't do this."

He can't come here and tell me not to go, not right now when I'm just about to leave. I've made up my mind. As much as I feel for him, this can never work. It's . . . too much. Too hard.

"Your dad called off the sale," he says, still trying to catch his breath fully.

"What?" My eyes dart to his. "Are you . . . he . . . what?"

I'm so confused. I can't even wrap my head around what he's just said.

"Sale? What's he talking about?" I hear Irene say behind me.

"He called it off?" I repeat.

Noel nods, his lips pulling into a full smile.

"But how do you know?" This all feels a little too good to be true.

"His attorney called my dad. Just a few minutes ago."

I don't know what to say. My dad came through. I honestly never thought he would. In every possible outcome to this situation, that was not the scenario I imagined would ever—could ever happen.

I drop my suitcase and my purse and basically throw myself into Noel's arms. He pulls me to him, my feet leaving the ground as he does. We're both laughing, and I can hear Hattie and Irene clapping behind us. They don't even know what they're cheering for.

I pull my head back as my feet hit the ground. "So, wait . . . what's happening with the land, then?"

Noel smiles. "I talked to my dad. He's going to let David Bersham buy it."

"Really?"

"Yep." He bobs his head up and down. "You did this. You saved us."

"No," I say. "It wasn't me. I just wanted to help."

"I'm so confused," says Hattie from behind me.

Noel chuckles and looks over my shoulder, keeping his arms tight around me. "I'll explain it all later," he says.

He brings his face back to mine. "This is . . . the best news," I say to him.

His face morphs into something more serious, his eyes focused on mine. "Stay," he says. "Don't leave—not yet, at least. Stay here a little longer. Please. Spend Christmas with me."

"Oh, yes," says Irene from behind me. "Please stay. You can even have your room back."

Noel gives me pleading eyes. "Please," he says again.

I could stay; I have nothing I need to be home for. There are still a lot of other barricades in our way, despite what happened with the land. This could complicate things.

I give him a serious look. "I don't know," I say. "I'm not sure I can spend Christmas with a bumpkin."

His lips pull up into a smile. Full and broad. Dimples and all. "I'll work on trying not to be such a bumpkin."

"You two," Hattie says. "You're under the mistletoe."

We both look up, at the stem of green leaves and red berries hanging from the top of the doorframe, in the exact place we met.

"Yeah, kiss already," says Irene.

"It's tradition," I say to Noel as I lean in, taking in his scruffy jaw and his spicy sent.

"Yes, it is," he says.

Epilogue

One year later: Christmas Day

"Listen up, everyone," says Mayor Holiday, making a clanking sound, tapping a knife to his water glass. He's standing at the end of a massive table, all of us surrounding it, waiting to eat the meal Veronica has put together. She hardly let anyone help her, though we all offered.

Christopher looks around the table and then lifts his champagne glass. "To family," he says. "New family," he says when he sees me. I smile brightly and then look down at the ring on my finger. Noel asked me to marry him last summer, while we were standing outside of his nearly finished house. I said yes, of course. We made it all official just a couple of days ago here in Carole Cove, with our family and friends surrounding us. Cami was my maid of honor, and Pete was Noel's best man. It was the most perfect, overdecorated wedding, thanks to Irene and Hattie, and I loved every second of it. Especially when Noel promised to drive me to Target at least once a month in his vows. I'll be holding him to that. Tomorrow, we leave for our honeymoon in the Virgin Islands.

"Old friends," Christopher says, continuing his speech, with an incline of his head toward David Bersham, who's sitting at the other end of the table, his wife next to him. David returns the gesture, their old rivalry a thing of the past. They finally put it behind them.

The new additions to Carole Cove, while not completely finished, have already brought more tourism to the area. Since making the town my permanent residence at the end of February, I've overseen nearly every part of it, working on the build-out and making all David's ideas come to life. It is, hands down, the best job I've ever had.

"New friends," says Christopher, with another nod, this time toward my mom and dad, who are sitting next to me. I look at them and smile. My dad looks at my mom and puts an arm around her. There's love there I've never seen before. My dad has done a full one-eighty; he's changed his ways. It took a lot of work on his part and a lot of forgiveness on ours, but he's a changed man. I'm so grateful my parents have this second chance. They were here for the wedding, and the Holidays' invited them to stay for Christmas. They invited Ben to stay too, but he had to head back home (to one that's void of Claudia, I might add).

"Family members who haven't quite joined us yet," Christopher says as chuckles filter through the room and all eyes land on Ivy, who's got Pete next to her, an arm around her shoulders, her hand resting on her ever-growing belly. It's a boy, which is just what Kaden wanted for Christmas this year.

"We're happy you're all here, celebrating with us," says Christopher. "So, before we dig in, I just want to say merry

Christmas to all of you, and may this next year be the best one yet."

We all lift our drinks, saying, "Hear! Hear!"

The room bursts with laughter and chatting after the speech, with everyone filling plates and passing dishes.

I look to Noel, and he leans in and places a kiss on my lips. I'm the happiest I've ever been, sitting in this room with everyone, next to the man I get to spend my life with. Surrounded by family in my own happily ever after, this all feels a lot like a scene straight out of one of those cheesy Christmas movies I still like to make fun of.

I wouldn't have it any other way.

THE END

About the Author

Becky Monson is a mother of three and a wife to one but would ditch them all for Henry Cavill. She used to write at night but now she's too dang tired, so she fits in writing between driving kids around to activities and running a household. With a talent for procrastination, Becky finds if she doesn't watch herself, she can waste an entire afternoon binge-watching Netflix. She's a USA Today bestseller and an award-winning author, and when she does actually get off Netflix to write, she uses humor and true life experiences to bring her characters to life.

Becky wishes she had a British accent and a magic spell to do her laundry. She has been trying to give up Diet Coke for the past ten years but has failed miserably.

Connect with Becky: www.beckymonson.com

Made in the USA
Monee, IL
08 December 2021